SUPER

Praise for *Super*

'A gorgeously written, powerfully rendered novel of migration, striving, hopes and dreams. Lindsay Pereira's world is deeply moving and hard to leave.'

—Sonia Faleiro

'Deeply empathetic and eerily unsettling, *Super* unpicks in forensic detail the makings and aftermath of the migration dream, and the price it extracts from the youth.'

—Santanu Bhattacharya

'Lindsay Pereira's deep dive into the world of Indian immigrants to Canada proves once again his claims to being one of India's most interesting and daring novelists. These lost lives are limned with empathy and touched by grace.'

—Jerry Pinto

SUPER

a novel

Lindsay Pereira

FOURTH ESTATE · *New Delhi*

First published in India by Fourth Estate 2026
An imprint of HarperCollins *Publishers*
HarperCollins *Publishers* India, Cyber City,
Building 10-A, Gurugram, Haryana – 122002, India
www.harpercollins.co.in

2 4 6 8 10 9 7 5 3 1

P-ISBN: 978-93-6569-926-5
E-ISBN: 978-93-6569-616-5

Typeset in 11.5/16.2 Sabon LT Std
by HarperCollins *Publishers* India Pvt. Ltd

Printed and bound at
Manipal Technologies Limited, Manipal

MIX
Paper | Supporting responsible forestry
FSC www.fsc.org FSC™ C043100

This book is produced from independently certified FSC® paper to ensure responsible forest management.

HarperCollins *Publishers*, Macken House, 39/40 Mayor Street Upper,
Dublin 1, D01 C9W8, Ireland

For Zarya, as always

and for
Hrisha Das

'We were terrified of the cold land
and the large amount of snow,
where people were different
and spoke a foreign language.'

—Anonietta Lanni nee Venditti,
'Italian Trunk',
Canadian Museum of Immigration at Pier 21,
Nova Scotia, Canada

TORONTO

12 SEPTEMBER 2019

Sukhpreet Gill's last day began with the kind of sunshine he had finally grown accustomed to. It was not the harsh, robust light that had blanketed the years of his childhood; that could sharply delineate green fields stretching into the distance. This was more like a radiance that made the leaves glow as if they were lit up by something behind them.

He breathed in deeply and rubbed his eyes, then coughed. The air was not as fresh as he would have wanted it to be, given the room's single window overlooking a parking lot. He liked beginning the day with breathing exercises, a habit acquired from his father who would spend his waking moments filling his lungs and exhaling vigorously. He wished he could have been around long enough for Sukhpreet to ask why, but his father had gone by the time he turned seven, and all he remembered of him was a crumpled body carried home by neighbours, the memory punctuated by his mother's unfettered howls of grief.

The condominium he shared with three other young men was quiet. It was a two-bedroom place in a less crowded part of Brampton, avoiding the crush of international students in the more popular areas. It had been chosen by him and his cousin in the hope that they could both save towards renting a place of their own in a few years. College in Jalandhar had taught him how to live with roommates, and his current lot were often up and away before he was, or asleep after a night shift, making it easier for him to use the kitchen and bathroom. These were small blessings, but he knew they were blessings, nonetheless.

Sitting up, he closed his eyes and recited the Japji Sahib, another ritual that came from his parents, and from their parents before them. There is only one god, he whispered, and truth is his name. His lips moved soundlessly through the rest of the prayer. When he was done, he shuffled his feet, feeling for a pair of rubber slippers cast on the floor the night before.

It was 6 a.m., and he should have been up a half hour ago, but it was also Thursday, and he expected few visitors at the superintendent's office. There could be complaints, but they would be on paper, deposited through a letterbox attached to the door. Tenants only dropped by in person on weekends, when they had the luxury of loitering for a while, protected from the demands of commuting to work or transporting children to school. Thursdays were always uneventful, and he relished the day, thankful for the solitude that would cocoon him as he went about his chores. The stairways had to be mopped, he remembered, and there was a dryer that needed to be checked before he could file an official complaint with the manufacturer.

He walked to the bathroom and splashed his face with warm water. It still delighted him, switching from ice cold to piping hot with a turn of the faucet. It always made him think of his mother, and how different her life could have been if they had had such easy access to water while growing up. He remembered her staggering home with two clay pots, the water drawn from their village well, one on each hip. She would walk in as slowly as possible to prevent spillage, then place one pot on the kerosene-powered stove and another on their mud floor. The water would take thirty minutes to boil, after which it would be poured into a plastic bucket with some cold water. They would use the bucket in turns, washing their faces before sitting down to breakfast. It felt like a lifetime ago, although it couldn't have been more than a decade since he had last done it.

Sighing, he turned off the faucet. He didn't like beginning the day with thoughts of his mother, because it made him melancholy. It made him think of Punjab, and what he had left behind. He was here, in Brampton, with a job that had taken over a year to find. To think of home now was an act of cowardice. Shaking his head, as if to dislodge an unwelcome thought, he wiped his face and walked out towards the kitchen. Placing a steel tumbler of water on the stovetop, he waited for it to boil, while trying to imagine the look on Ma's face when she could finally visit him.

He had been promising to bring her for a while now, but ticket prices had only risen, and he was still uncertain of whether she would be granted a tourist visa. There was nothing either of them could do but be patient until he had enough for her ticket. Air Canada was ruthless, but he expected nothing else from this country. 'Let them raise prices again,' he muttered, 'let them raise it as much as they want, and I will still bring her.' He stared at the tumbler with unseeing eyes as the water began to bubble. When he had added milk powder and tea leaves, he opened the refrigerator and removed two slices of bread from a packet, carefully inserting them into the toaster. He watched as the bars began to glow, toasting the bread unevenly on both sides. There would be nothing else until lunch, and he wished someone could cook him a parantha and serve it with dahi.

Pulling up a plastic chair, he sat at the table purchased from IKEA and chewed the bread slowly, dipping each slice into the tea he had strained. He thought of the buns back home, sliced and slathered thickly with butter, and wished he didn't have to deal with these recurring moments of gloom that ambushed him. He wanted to look to the future, not the past, because all he had there was his mother and a world of sadness. It should have had no hold over him, and yet it did, for reasons he couldn't explain. Enough, he said to himself. Enough. Swallowing the last of his tea, he took the mug and plate to the sink, rinsing both before placing them on a plastic mat to dry.

He thought about Harneet. It was around 4.00 p.m. in Jalandhar, which meant she would be at work. It was a call centre, where employees weren't allowed to carry phones, so messaging her was pointless. If it were a weekend, he would have asked her to step outside for a chat, but she wouldn't get her phone until the shift ended at 6 p.m., so he sent her an emoji—a kiss—on WhatsApp, then switched to YouTube.

His favourite song this month was 'Toronto Wala Gabhru' by a singer who, he had been delighted to find out, was from Brampton. Sukhpreet smiled, thinking about the city mentioned in the song, and what living there had taught him. Still, it was a good tune, so he hummed along, as he pulled off his shirt and prepared to take a shower. '*Unjh gharon jaan ni dinde*,' he sang, '*jana Jassi kole ehi kehke ajungi*.' It amused him, this endless stream of music about life in the West. Back in Jalandhar, the songs had sustained him, occupying waking hours and listless nights with visions of bright lights and buildings that nuzzled the sky. They conjured a world that made it easier for him to cope with the one he was living in. He should have outgrown such visions, now that he had seen these streets and knew what went into the maintenance of these buildings. And yet, he thought, maybe he still listened to that music because it reminded him of the boy he had been when a promising future still beckoned.

One of the bedroom doors was closed, which meant someone was asleep. The rest of the condominium was empty, so he turned the music up a little louder as he pulled on his shoes. He continued to whistle as he walked out and down the stairs. Getting to work would take a little over an hour and a half, unless he missed his GO train, which had happened just once. Once in the city, it was a short ride by bus from the train station to the building where he worked.

The superintendent's office had to be open by 9 a.m., but he liked getting there earlier whenever possible, sitting by himself in the empty room and imagining the tenants still asleep, sorting through their complaints, or reading notices from the Beltway Properties head office. The office occupied a small corner of the lobby at 640 Rosebud Avenue, where he worked as an assistant to the superintendent. On some mornings, he looked up from his desk and wondered how someone from Jalandhar could be hired to manage a seven-storey building in midtown Toronto. It was his responsibility to make sure it was clean, that renovations were carried out on time, and that the pipes functioned smoothly through all kinds of weather. It was the possibility of being placed in charge of the budget that impressed him most, of being able to tell the head office that a contractor would paint the premises for a fee, while knowing that his recommendations would be accepted.

His bus stopped a few feet from the building. Humming softly again, he unlocked the office, turning on a portable black fan stacked on top of two cardboard boxes. He liked the gently clicking sound it made while he worked, reminding him of years in classrooms cooled by fans that hung from long, steel rods. Another reason he liked coming in early was because it allowed him to get comfortable with the desktop computer. All communication with the head office was via email, but he still struggled with basics like attachments. Switching on the machine, he double-clicked the Chrome icon and logged on to YouTube once more, this time to a tutorial on Microsoft Outlook. He watched for ten minutes, pausing, then replaying sections.

At 9 a.m., he stopped the video and shut the browser. The first task on his list was a walk around the building and parking lot. He had to check for unlisted vehicles parked overnight, then make his way to the basement closet for cleaning supplies. He nodded at the Filipino lady, who stood at the building's entrance. She was a nurse, which he respected. They saw each other often in the mornings as she waited for her bus. The stop was on the opposite side of the street, but she preferred waiting in the building. It had been almost four months since he had been hired, but he hadn't exchanged a word with her. Maybe she didn't speak English, he thought, or maybe she assumed he didn't. He knew she wouldn't understand his accent but hoped he would be able to articulate himself better in the months to come.

Walking past her, he made his way slowly around the building, stepping over grass that had begun to dry. It was September and the temperature had begun to drop. In two weeks, he would have to supervise leaf blowers and make sure the falling leaves were removed. There had been an email from the office about a ban on gas-powered leaf blowers. There were six complaints last fall, apparently, from tenants who couldn't stand the noise. He also knew they would complain if they found leaves on the premises, and it surprised him, this misplaced anger that raised its head now and again, from people who had so much but couldn't find it within themselves to be happy. So what if the leaf blowers made a noise? Did they know what a noisy city was really like? He had smiled while reading the email, imagining the shock on their faces if they were to visit Jalandhar, a city so consumed with activity that silence often felt like an act of violence.

Around him, parents and children made their way to the nearest school, North Prep Elementary. He liked watching them go by, painting pictures in his head of a time when he and Harneet would have children of their own. Would they live in this part of Toronto? He didn't think they would, but imagined his children growing up in Canada, thinking of this country as their own. He wondered what that felt like for those who had been born here and took so much for granted. Did they wake up every morning like he still did, rubbing their eyes and reminding themselves of where they were?

A large black squirrel ran past him and up a tree, and he followed its rapid ascent. When he first arrived, he would take pictures of these creatures, delighted at seeing them run so freely. He recalled video calls with Harneet, showing her squirrels chasing each other, and they would laugh. It sometimes felt as if he had been living in Canada for years, although it hadn't been that long since he arrived at Pearson. He missed Jalandhar, his mother and Harneet, but they all knew what it meant for him to be here, and what they would all have to sacrifice until they saw each other again.

Suddenly upset, he looked away from the children, turning at a corner of the building towards the parking lot. Someone had thrown away an empty box of pizza and two cups of Coke. They must have thrown it from their balconies, and it annoyed him, this refusal to use bins. There was a chute on each floor, which they could use, but he knew this wasn't about cleanliness. It was about privilege, and the ability to throw something from balconies if they wanted to, because there would always be someone ready to clean up their mess; they paid rent and knew that it included maintenance.

He bent down and picked up the empty box and cups, carrying them to a large plastic bin. It had a 'City of Toronto' stamp, and wheels, and it had to be moved down to the curb once a week, where a truck would empty it. The stink of garbage didn't distract him from how marvellous the system was. He knew Canada's streets looked worse as one moved away from the city and into the suburbs, but it was still one of the things he liked to tell Harneet and his mother about, revelling in their undivided attention as he spoke with new authority about this country that was now home.

Walking away from the parking lot, he made his way back to the office, knowing the supervisor would be there soon. He was a large Colombian man named Diego, and Sukhpreet had liked him from the moment they met at his job interview. 'Indian and Colombian are like Cola-Cola and ice,' he had said, an expression that made no sense to Sukhpreet, but which he had laughed at, because he felt that the man was friendly. He thought about it later, what Diego had meant to convey, and whether he should have asked for an explanation. Eventually, he let it go, because his boss was a kind, decent man. That was all that mattered, after the warnings he had been given about being exploited. Diego trusted him, which meant more than anything else.

The Filipino lady had left by the time he got back to the entrance. There was a large truck near the spot where he had last seen her, filled with the belongings of a tenant moving in. He walked up to the driver's side and tapped the door lightly, looking up at the window a foot above. The driver's head appeared, a white man with a Blue Jays cap. He looked down, saying nothing.

'Sir, no trucks allowed until 10 a.m.,' Sukhpreet said, pointing to a sign in the lobby that neither he nor the driver could read from this distance.

'What?'

'No trucks, sir,' Sukhpreet repeated, aware of his accent. 'We are allowing tenants to bring belongings only between ten in the morning and twelve in the afternoon.'

'What do you mean? No one told me anything about timings. We've driven down from Hamilton and I'm going nowhere. I have to drop this off and get back.'

'Sorry, sir. Building rules. Come back at 10 a.m. only. Just forty-five minutes to go.'

The man looked as if he were about to say something, then stopped himself and glared at Sukhpreet, who smiled nervously. He hoped Diego would step outside and sort this out because he never knew what to expect from white people. The building's Caucasian tenants were usually polite, but never looked him in the eye, and it felt as if they interacted with him only because they had no choice. He knew the driver didn't like him, and that he wasn't saying anything because he wanted to swallow the anger that had emerged, unbidden, between them. They both knew it was easier to abuse a brown man than to fight authority, and Sukhpreet braced himself. It would take a half hour for Diego to materialize; all he could do was pacify the man and hope he would move.

'Sorry, sir,' he said again. 'I am only an assistant.'

'What do I do about that?'

'My boss will not let me change the rule, sir. You have to come back at ten.'

Looking down at Sukhpreet again, his lips curled in distaste. 'You people,' he said, then muttered under his breath. Slapping the dashboard in frustration, he turned the ignition key and began to move slowly out of the driveway. As he turned into the main street, Sukhpreet let out a deep breath he didn't recall holding. He swallowed, then walked into the building, his ears still tuned to the sound of the truck pulling away.

He wished his job didn't involve speaking with people. It was never a problem at home because he thought of himself as a friendly person with a convincing manner. That belief in his ability to be a great salesperson had been repeatedly tested and found wanting, from the time he arrived at the immigration desk at Pearson airport, to his interactions with cashiers at the local No Frills store. Few of the people he interacted with understood what he was saying, even though he spoke as slowly and carefully as possible. They would stare in incomprehension, then wait for him to repeat himself, and it always made him feel as if he was in their way, some mysterious obstacle placed there to make their lives harder. It made him feel guilty at the time, then angry, because he didn't know where the guilt was coming from. It was tiring, and he dreaded it, even as he knew how unavoidable it was if he needed to keep working.

There were more people in the lobby now, tenants who recognized him and nodded. They would greet him on some days and look through him when they were in a hurry, and he had learned not to take it personally. They had no interest in who he was, only in what he represented as an employee of a firm that offered them housing. They turned to him when the dryers stopped working, or when someone dropped a half-eaten ice cream cone in an elevator.

He walked into the office and picked up a key for the janitor's closet. Mopping was one of the tasks he had grown to appreciate, despite never having cleaned a room before. Now, he had learned how to position his shoulders, and to avoid corners. 'If they can't see it, they don't think about it,' Diego had told him early on, after spotting Sukhpreet struggling to move a vending machine in the laundry room so he could mop beneath it. From then on, he had tried to look at every task from Diego's perspective, doing what was visible, ignoring what no one would see.

Mopping had begun to take on a meditative aspect, allowing him to move from floor to floor, like a ghost, thinking about everything or nothing. It made him feel like a monk, like someone who had renounced everything that once moved him, as if he had replaced the young man he was with an older person whose hopes and dreams were more tempered. It was also a way of avoiding conversation, however cursory. Even saying, 'Have a nice day' was hard, because he came from a country where no one used those words, and where friendly greetings to strangers were treated with suspicion. There, one simply went about one's business; forced civilities were a luxury reserved for the rich.

Walking to the elevator, he pressed the button for the basement, where a closet held a mop, bucket and cleaning supplies. There was also a tap. Filling the bucket with hot water, he opened a bottle of industrial cleaning liquid and poured out a little. It was supposed to smell like citrus, but there was a chemical aroma that overpowered all other scents. It was fragrance without nuance, something functional meant to convey to those who could smell it that this was done for their benefit: a place had been sterilized and cleaned, so they could feel safer. Diego had asked him to wear rubber gloves, warning him that the liquid could leave his hands raw, but Sukhpreet hated the gloves. They felt like unwanted skin, so he mopped without them, humming when he was sure there was no one around to hear him.

Carrying the bucket with his left hand, and mop in his right, he headed back to the elevator, planning to start on the highest floor and work his way down. Diego would be in by the time he finished, and he could give him a report of what he had seen or inform him of anything that needed fixing. The lift stopped just once, on the ground floor, and two tenants stepped inside. They stopped speaking when they noticed him, then nodded by way of greeting. Stepping off on the fourth floor, they walked out and picked up the conversation they had abandoned, forgetting to wish him a good day. He thought about whether he should have said something, then caught himself thinking of how absurd it was, the idea of worrying over whether he should have greeted them or not. How did it matter when they were all playing roles assigned to them for as long as they occupied these premises?

The elevator stopped at the seventh floor, and he stepped out, picking up the bucket and setting it down gingerly. Much of the floor was covered by a grey rug that was cleaned twice a year by contractors, but the stairways and space outside each elevator needed to be mopped weekly. Dipping the mop into the bucket, he swirled it around a few times, then wiped the space outside the elevators. When he was done, he picked up the bucket and walked to a door leading to the stairway, pushing it open with his shoulder. There were no tenants about, which was usually the case at this hour. It sometimes made him feel as if the building was empty, even though he knew there were no vacancies except for the person moving in later that morning.

Humming again, he sloshed the mop around and began wiping down the stairs mechanically, slowly getting into a rhythm. The water began to turn brown, soapsuds floating at the top. The smell of disinfectant was strong, and he closed his eyes for a second, leaning against the wall, before starting again. He was almost at the fifth floor now, and heard the stairway door open a floor below, followed by the sound of someone coming up the stairs. He stopped, waiting until the person had walked past and stepped out into the passageway behind him. He seemed like an older man, but Sukhpreet couldn't be sure, because he had a red hoodie on, with a blue cap pulled down low over his face. As he rounded the stairs, Sukhpreet leaned back to make way. He didn't notice the knife until it was inside him, slipping below his ribcage on the left, just below the breastbone.

'You people should fucking die,' the man said, softly, as if he were asking for directions.

There was pain, but Sukhpreet couldn't register the source or its intensity, because the overwhelming feeling was one of surprise. He looked down upon a hand that still held the knife. It had slid through his shirt cleanly, and there was a wetness that he didn't think of as blood. The hand was white. It was a white man. And then, he found himself falling. He opened his mouth to scream, but the man had pulled out the knife and stabbed him again, this time in the chest, again to his left. Now there was pain, a keen sense of it, as if he was being plunged into ice cold water, and he felt something scrape past bone, leaving him breathless. It hurt like nothing he could recall, and he felt as if he were standing on a tall platform, looking down upon this attack unfolding beneath. I'm dying, he thought, I am going to die. This man is trying to kill me.

He felt a hand on his mouth, a palm pressed against his lips as if to force back any words threatening to spill through. It was harder to breathe, and he kicked out, feeling his right leg push against the bucket that moved a few inches, the water inside sloshing without spilling. He kicked again, this time with both legs, arms reaching for his attacker as he tried to push away the hand, but he didn't feel strong enough and started to cry. This wasn't how it was supposed to end, he thought, not like this, not after everything. There were fleeting thoughts about his mother, and Harneet, and lines of songs he hadn't sung in years, and an image of startled sparrows flying away from a field like a cloud slowly imploding.

There were black spots in front of his eyes now, and he blinked, screaming weakly into the man's hand. He tried moving towards the door, but it was too far away, and he realized he had slipped closer to the edge of the stairs. The man pulled out the knife one more time and stabbed him, this time in the stomach. Sukhpreet opened his eyes wide, then felt them start to close of their own volition. He could no longer push, and felt his right hand fall limply beside him. The man finally removed his hand and stood up; the front of his hoodie wet with blood that looked like water. Was this why he had worn something red, Sukhpreet wondered, his last thought before his eyes closed and he felt a blackness fall upon them like a blanket.

He sensed his body being moved, slowly, but couldn't open his eyes. He was pushed closer to the stairway, and fell, rolling over one, then two stairs, tumbling as if in slow motion, until he reached the bottom and stopped. His breath felt shallow. He opened his dry mouth to call out to his mother, but she wasn't here. She was far away, in another country, where the only other person he loved was at work, waiting for him to send her a message.

There was silence in the stairway as he died, his attacker looking down from the top of the stairs before pushing open the door and vanishing into the corridor. A few floors below, Diego opened the door to the superintendent's office and stepped inside, noting the absence of the bucket as he sat down and saw the papers that Sukhpreet had printed for his attention. He took the phone and called the head office, informing them that one of the dryers had broken down again. Then, when he had looked through the other complaints, he walked out of the office, pulling the door shut behind him.

JALANDHAR

10 FEBRUARY 2015

What would Rainak Bazar look like without its crush of people, Harneet Kaur wondered, as she often did on Friday evenings when she walked the market's narrow streets towards an aloo tikki stall. It sometimes felt as if everyone in the state of Punjab chose to converge upon Ali Mohalla at the same time she did, even though she knew it was always this crowded, and far worse on weekends. What was harder to comprehend was the feeling that most people around her were shopping for a wedding. It was a fair assumption, given the number of clothing shops lining both sides of most streets, but it still amazed her, this relentless march towards marriage that appeared to consume her people.

There was no one with her this evening, which she preferred, not because she disliked her classmates but because their talk would inadvertently shift to questions about the International English Language Testing System, immigration agents, or the pros and cons of Brampton over Southall. She didn't want to talk about foreign countries; she just wanted her favourite snack.

There were sarees everywhere she looked, many flecked with sequins that glittered in the dust kicked up by scooters and mopeds, as drivers squeezed through the throng of pedestrians. She walked past Bombay Saree, then Lovely Best Price, and a shop called London Dreams, before the street curved gently at Saini Silks. Her tikkiwalla stood at a corner to the right, the oil from his large cast iron pan sputtering, as chillies were constantly thrown in along with potato patties. It was an indulgence she looked forward to at the end of every week.

Her bag felt heavier than usual because Fridays were when college was followed by two hours of practice tests for the IELTS. There were a lot of girls from her college, Kanya Maha Vidyalaya, who took the tests with her, but few had the patience for a walk to Rainak Bazar at the end of the day. For Harneet, it was not just a plate of tikki; it was a reminder that there was more to life than the endless pursuit of a way out of Jalandhar. There was always the nagging thought that nothing she learned, in college or outside, would affect the rest of her life. The only thing she had to do was use those years of study to find a way out, to another city or country far from her own. It was a message drilled into them all, the girls at KMV and the boys at DAV College, a silent rebuke that hung in the air, that to stay here longer than necessary was a prison sentence.

Accepting her plate of tikki from the vendor, she turned away from the street, in the hope that it would be slightly less dusty. It had been almost a year since she had begun stopping by, and it felt as if the vendor now recognized her, although there were hundreds of girls who stopped by through the week. He sometimes told her of his plans to move to a small shop where customers could sit at tables, but nothing had happened. She suspected it was a story he repeated to anyone who would listen, as if repeating it would manifest that dream. She had heard that he had occupied the corner for over a decade. His battered aluminium plates had stayed the same, a step above disposable plates made of palash leaves, but below the more expensive option of stainless steel. She humoured him, nodding as he spoke of renting a place not far from where they stood. Perhaps they both knew he would be here forever, his customers growing up and moving away, or coming back with children to be served by an older version of him.

It was one of the many things she loved about Jalandhar, how it made everyone want to move far away, while trying to hold on to everything they knew about the city. It felt like being tied to the place with a thread of gold, both fragile and unbreakable. Harneet was born here, as were her parents. They were the only ones in their large extended family who had stayed. Her aunts, uncles and cousins were now scattered across the globe, turning up only at weddings or funerals to talk about how she had grown, or to ask when she planned to marry. In a year or two, they would come bearing proposals from young men they knew in Birmingham and Vancouver, Auckland and Sydney, all raised to expect young Punjabi wives who would do their bidding and treat them the way their mothers had. It was something she didn't want to think about, even as she knew it was only a matter of time before it became the only thought she would have to consider.

It happened every Friday, her mind wandering down a path that was now predictable, ending with images of being stuck in an apartment in some Western city, preparing paranthas for uncaring children, her adult years spent shuffling between a kitchen and the local gurudwara. She wondered if she would recall the tikkiwalla in those moments and look upon these evenings with something like fondness. Swallowing the hot mix of potato, bread and tamarind chutney, she wished she could stay a while longer, for another plate, or for the promise of something other than an uneventful and silent weekend with her parents.

Home was quieter than it had been when she was a child, and she couldn't recall when that cloak of stillness had fallen upon the three of them. She knew her father and mother had begun to confront a future without her, their only child, and the possibility of seeing her once a year or less, depending upon the largesse of the family she married into. She resented the idea, but had long accepted it, because the love of her parents was weaker than their need to save face. Society demanded that young women leave to serve young men lucky enough to get away. To stay behind was to be condemned to a life with someone who had failed, and her parents would never be able to meet their relatives if that happened. They had raised her to believe she was bright, a virtue that celebrated as well as condemned her, and she had only begun to recognize it after moving to college, when the prospect of a life abroad was suddenly, and terrifyingly, made real.

She finished her tikki. Turning to return the plate, she was startled by a young man who was eating while facing her. He blushed, then apologized, saying he wasn't staring, and was only trying to protect his food from dust kicked up in the street. Harneet nodded, her mind still on the weekend. It hadn't occurred to her that he had been deliberately facing her, and she brushed off his apology the way she ignored any attention. He was obviously a DAV boy, one of those insecure youth who took it upon themselves to ride motorbikes in circles outside the entrance to KMV, whistling and singing to girls after classes ended at 3 p.m. Paying the vendor, she realized he was still speaking, and turned to look at him again.

He was slim, with a kind face, his moustache faint, as if pencilled in by a make-up artist. He wore a long-sleeved shirt and plain black turban. She thought a blue one would suit his angular face better, bringing out his sharp cheekbones, then checked herself for judging him.

'Were you saying something to me?' she asked, more roughly than she intended.

'I said sorry,' he replied. 'Sorry.'

'I heard you the first time. It's okay.'

She turned away to pocket her change.

'Are you from KMV?' he asked, prompting her to turn again. 'I am from DAV.'

There was something rustic about his Punjabi, an earthiness that betrayed his roots. It was not the sharper accent of Jalandhar and had a lilt that was almost musical. Despite herself, she felt as if she wanted to hear more, to have this stranger make her language feel new.

'I didn't ask where you were from,' she said, more politely this time. He smiled, then, and she found herself smiling back. How absurd it was, this interaction with a stranger, yet so comfortable, as if they were old friends meeting for a chat.

'I am Sukhpreet. Sukhpreet Gill. I only asked because I have heard things about KMV girls. I am not from Jalandhar.'

'I know you're not, and I don't know what you heard about KMV, but it's probably not true.'

She began to walk away as he handed over his empty plate to the vendor, along with a twenty-rupee note. She didn't turn, wondering if he would follow her, and thought about how she was behaving. This was not respectable at all, speaking with a young man, let alone a stranger.

'What is your name?' she heard him ask, from a step behind. 'I will stop walking if it bothers you, but I don't know anyone in Jalandhar, and I am only trying to know the city.'

She slowed down, giving him a chance to catch up, then looked at him. 'What do you want to know about Jalandhar, and where are you from?'

'Chukhiara.'

'Where is that?'

'Around 30 kilometres from here. Beautiful village.'

'Never heard of it.'

'There are fields, and wells, and no dust. It's not like here. It's super.'

'Then why did you come here?' she asked, annoyed at the perceived slight against her city.

'Why does anyone come to Jalandhar? Everything is here. Colleges, hospitals, so much to see. Imagine looking at fields every day of your life. How would that make you feel?'

'I don't know. I have never heard of Chukhiara, so how do I imagine what it feels like?'

They had reached the main road, and Harneet felt calm. She had never spoken to a man like this, but it felt safe. She knew it was irrational, given the reputation of DAV students, but he didn't come across as brash. There was a gentleness to his manner that made her feel like the stronger one. It was an unusual sensation. He was not weak, but there was a vulnerability in the way he spoke. She wondered if she was being naive, and if the hesitance with which he had approached her hid an ulterior motive. But they were still in a public place, and all he asked were questions about Jalandhar. What were the best places for paranthas? Where did young people go on weekends? Were there cheap hostels? Did students get discounts?

She answered patiently, wondering when he would ask her something more personal, but he didn't. He hadn't asked for her name again either, and she liked that, him treating her like a local with information to share, rather than as a young woman to impress. He said nothing about his own life, and she felt herself wanting to ask him, but stopped herself.

'I have to go,' she said, and he nodded.

'Do you like the tikki here?'

'I come every Friday to eat it.'

She didn't know, even as she said it, why she had offered that information.

'See you next Friday then,' he smiled, then walked away.

Harneet watched him for a few seconds until he disappeared into the crowd. She sensed that her mouth was open, as if she were about to smile, and looked around to see if there was anyone who recognized her. The sun had begun to set, and Rainak Bazar would soon light up, its sarees sparkling. She still had a ten-minute walk and picked up her pace as she headed to the bus stop.

She knew she should have left earlier because the buses were not as safe as they used to be. She wished she didn't feel so susceptible every Friday and blamed the gossip at college for making her feel this way. There was always some classmate talking about being harassed or followed. Harneet had never experienced the things they talked about but knew there was always a first time for something bad to happen. The bus took fifteen minutes to arrive, and she climbed in. It was full, but there were a few older men on board, which reassured her. She sometimes thought about women outside Jalandhar, in India and beyond. Did they also need this reassurance that there were older men to protect them from younger ones? When she was little, she thought of young men as romantic, the kind who would make college life magical. But after a year of lectures, all she had found in classrooms was a regular break from her parents.

There were a few empty seats, she noticed, moving towards one as the bus ran over a pothole. She sat down, guilty about the way she thought of her parents. She didn't doubt their love and knew how hard it was for them. But they had reconciled themselves to her absence a long time ago, while she was only just beginning to see what that meant. Her goals—to study, marry and leave—must have been etched, as if in stone, on the day she arrived at Cantonment General Hospital, eighteen years ago. Her story had always been known to them; it was she who had only just begun turning the pages.

She hated this train of thought because of how humdrum it was, week after week, as she made her way home. She didn't want to think of her uneventful past, or of a future that didn't gleam as brightly as she assumed it did for the girls in her class. They would stare at their phones for hours, sharing photographs of relatives or friends posing in front of some famous monument, in cities with unpronounceable names. The photographs always seemed staged, the smiles forced, and she felt like the odd one out. Was she a pessimist, condemned to grow older without enjoying any part of her own journey? Would it always be like this ride home, in one poorly maintained vehicle after another, with only the changing facades of stores outside marking time as life slipped past?

The light was starting to fade as she stepped off the bus and began walking towards her building. There were newer towers coming up, and she read their names on large boards outside each construction site: Sunny Prime Enclave, Hamilton Tower, Eldeco Estate Club, Khurana Complex. They announced homes for sale or rent, promising lifestyles at odds with their surroundings. The advertisements showed fair young men lounging alongside pools, and women in tights on treadmills. Where were these people in Jalandhar? Were they leaving their homes in Bombay and Delhi to move here? No one she knew looked like this, so who were the towers for?

Her own building was modest and old, built almost three decades ago. It would vanish too, replaced by a township neither of her parents would adjust to, assuming they could still afford to stay on. The thought of them growing old here was almost too much to bear on some days, when she considered how faraway they expected her to go. Why was she never encouraged to live in Jalandhar? Why the emphasis on going abroad, as if there were no options? Hadn't her parents lived here all their lives? Had it been so miserable? What weren't they telling her about their past, and what were they trying to protect her from? There were no luxuries, but they had been happy, and that ought to have been enough. A sudden wave of exhaustion overwhelmed her.

Turning into her compound, she was struck by how the only people she came across here were old. They would sit outside for hours on benches made of crumbling concrete that had been placed there years ago with money collected from all the residents. There were no young people, just parents and grandparents who would disappear for months at a time, visiting children abroad, then return to haunt the building until their next trip.

'Sat Sri Akal,' she greeted them as she passed, making her way to the stairs. They nodded, watching her, and she could feel the heat of their gaze as she disappeared up the stairwell. They were evaluating how old she was, and how long she could stay single, and she knew they would have those conversations with her parents whenever they stepped outside. It saddened her because she could imagine her parents doing the same thing decades from now, on a bench, speaking to neighbours as old as they were, with nothing to look forward to except the gurudwara and a holiday to visit her, if the man she eventually married would agree to let them come and stay a while.

She climbed up to the second floor and stopped outside her apartment. She often waited there, as if summoning up some reserve of strength without knowing why she needed it. She knocked, and her father opened the door. The room smelled of onion and turmeric; dinner was almost ready. She could hear her mother in the kitchen, and the soft sizzle that accompanied the pressing down of a parantha on a hot tava. She loved it when a teaspoon of butter was tapped onto the parantha after it was done, the aroma transporting her to her schooldays, when she was a spoiled child they had doted on.

She never doubted that her parents cared. What she saw on their faces now was fear. She had always thought of them as strong people who loved each other unconditionally, but had increasingly begun to see them for who they were: a couple condemned to grow old alone. She wished again, as she often had, for a sibling; a brother, perhaps, who could give them hope and something to look forward to. Nothing she said or did could come close, and this made it hard for her to smile when she was around them.

Placing her bag on a chair, she walked into the bathroom and splashed cold water on her face before entering the kitchen. Her mother turned and smiled, informing her that dinner would be served in ten minutes.

'What did you study today?' her father asked, putting aside his copy of *Ajit*, the Punjabi newspaper delivered to every home in the building. He used to read it to her as a child, patiently correcting her as she stumbled over the words in Gurmukhi, and she found it amusing to repeat the exercise in reverse these days as they both read *The Tribune*. She liked the English language, but wondered if she would have the confidence to carry out a conversation with a native speaker. Even their English teacher at college struggled, switching to Hindi while trying to explain the difference between words like 'affect' and 'effect'.

'History of India,' she replied, waiting for him to ask what period they had chosen. She wanted to tell him it was about the Portuguese rule but knew he would be more excited if she mentioned the British, or World War II, both topics he could talk about for hours if he were to find a receptive audience. He would mention the soldiers in his family, how mothers would have three sons and assume that two would never come home, how his grandfather had reappeared fifteen years after the Partition to find that his wife had not remarried. She sensed that those memories made him feel larger, if only for a while, part of something other than his small family in this crumbling apartment. As a child, she felt his pride and shared it, and he would hoist her on his shoulders as they ran from the living room to the single bedroom, firing imaginary pistols at British soldiers from behind tables and cupboards. She thought about the last time he had carried her, years ago, even as he began speaking about Jallianwala Bagh and asking if her teacher had told them the whole story.

Her mother interrupted them with a call to dinner. She had two steel thalis with paranthas and a bowl of dal on each. Harneet waited until she joined them with her own thali, and her father said a short prayer before they began to eat. She listened as they spoke of a society meeting to address the problem of someone's pet Alsatian, what a doctor on television had said about drinking warm water after a meal, and who had managed to secure a visa. They would soon ask about her own plans, and if she had an idea of where she wanted to apply after her bachelor's.

She had a few years to go, but knew she would have to come up with a sensible response soon. It had been on their minds for a while, her moving abroad on a student visa, or marrying someone who was already a British or Canadian citizen.

'Lots of universities in New Zealand want Indian students this year,' her mother said, looking to her husband for confirmation.

He nodded. 'You just need a good IELTS score, and half your problems are gone,' he said, looking up at her.

'I am doing practice tests,' she said, hoping they would stop discussing it.

'Listen to English news channels before bed,' her father said. 'And go to Mr Malhotra's house in the B Wing on Saturday. I have spoken to him, and his son left some notes behind before he left for Auckland.'

'A good boy,' her mother added. 'Did Malhotra say anything about his marriage plans?'

'What plans?' Harneet asked. 'Are you discussing my marriage?'

'No, beta,' her father said, 'I am just asking around to see what the neighbours are saying about the best place for proposals. The UK is asking for too much proof these days, so I just ...'

'Let it be, Papaji,' she interrupted. 'We can ask when it's time to discuss marriage. Why now?'

He laughed. 'You can't wait until later, beta. If we wait until it is too late, all the good boys will be taken, and then where will you go?'

She stopped chewing and looked at him. 'Why do you always want me to go? Why do you never want me to stay?'

He turned away and said nothing. Her mother was quiet, too, and they ate in silence. Harneet waited until her father had finished, then picked up his thali along with her own. She walked to the kitchen and placed the dishes in the sink, turning the faucet and watching water splash on the thalis.

There was still an hour to go before bed. Harneet thought about the weekend, and the classes she had to attend the next morning. She had English from 1 p.m. until 4 p.m. on

Saturdays, and assignments for college that would have to be done on Sunday. It felt relentless, this need to constantly better herself for something or, more specifically, someone. It made her feel like the goats she sometimes passed on the way to KMV, raised in makeshift camps along the side of the road, transported from one location to another, wherever grass was available, until they were slaughtered, their meat parcelled out in small plastic bags.

She had wanted to study for as long as she could remember, but this didn't feel like an education. It felt like preparation for something nameless, not the pursuit of knowledge that would lead to a purer outcome, something beneficial to her life and soul. If only she could have studied medicine or law. She knew, even if she hated both subjects, that to study them would make her feel like a different person, more in control of her destiny. She didn't blame her parents because she sensed they would have allowed her to study whatever she chose, if only she were vocal about it. She had only herself to blame, and this enervating fog in which she grew up, and this locality that struck down any girl who dared to stand and stare anyone in the eye. It was the people she grew up with who made it impossible for young women to walk down paths not created by others before them.

Drying her hands on a washcloth, she walked out of the kitchen and into the living room. Her mother still sat at the dining table, her hands greasy, an empty plate before her. She looked up at Harneet and smiled. Her father was on the sofa, part of a set with two bulky chairs, all positioned in a semicircle around their LG colour television. The news was on, with the volume low, transforming the anchor's voice into a mild drone, like that of a fly buzzing against a windowpane.

'Did you stop by your tikkiwala again?' he asked, smiling. 'Why don't you bring us back some?'

'It gets soggy too quickly,' she replied, sitting down beside him, and leaning into his shoulder. It was one of her favourite things to do—burrowing into his skin and shutting the world outside for a few moments. He reached out with his right arm and enveloped her.

'You really like that tikkiwala. What is wrong with the food in your college canteen?'

'Nothing, but his aloo tikki is the best in Jalandhar.'

'I haven't been to Rainak Bazar since your cousin got married,' he said, turning to his wife. 'Was that two years ago?'

'Almost three now,' Harneet's mother replied.

'Where are they now? How many children?'

'Some city called Surrey in Canada. She had a son last year, but they haven't come to visit. I should call her mother.'

Harneet listened to them gossip about family and friends, their children and grandchildren. She remembered some of them, but most were just faceless entities—people supposedly related, who would forever feel like strangers, unless she ended up on their shores. If that happened, she knew how much she would have to work to rekindle those bonds, to immerse herself into the minutiae of their lives, in the hope that they would let her back in. The only time she met her cousins, aunts or uncles was when someone got married or passed away. There were no conversations, no exchanges of personal information.

A lot had to do with choices made by her father, his dismissal from the army due to poor health, followed by his career as a teller at Punjab National Bank. It was looked down upon, his refusal to get out of this city. It was made to feel like failure, as if growing old in the place of one's birth was a crime. She often thought about where that need to flee came from, the restlessness that prevented her relatives from settling down and breathing in the dust of their ancestors. Didn't they see that everything they needed was in the one place they were constantly encouraged to leave?

She yawned, suddenly tired, then realized she still had three pages of writing to complete before class the following afternoon. They had been tasked with completing an essay on women's safety, and it had amused her, that they were to address a problem that had never been deemed important enough to be resolved. Everyone knew about how hard it was for women to walk down the streets after dark. No one said a word about the men in SUVs, addled by drugs or alcohol, threatening to pick up any girl who happened to find herself out alone.

She wanted to write about the men of Jalandhar and how they would turn the same subject around to talk about propriety, and how everyone would reiterate that women belonged indoors. Men never considered the irony of the classes her classmates attended, and the hope that English would propel them into countries where women were encouraged to step out and take control. She hoped they would leave their ideas about traditional roles behind, but doubted it. They would get student visas and go out into the wide world, forever carrying a little piece of darkness with them, no matter how brightly the lights outside twinkled.

JALANDHAR

17 AUGUST 2015

The assistant wasn't looking up at him. Sukhpreet tried raising his voice a little, then lowered it almost instantly, worried about coming across as rude. There were around forty other men behind him, patiently waiting their turn at the counter. It had taken him five weeks to get an appointment and he wanted to convince the woman behind the counter that his application was genuine. Her name was Rita, and he couldn't tell if she was Punjabi because there was no last name on the plastic tag affixed to the front of her blouse.

It was 12.45 p.m., and he had already been here for four hours. He knew the assistants were overworked and would probably dismiss him within minutes, moving on to the next student if he wasn't good enough to be assigned an education counsellor. The centre was called Student Abroad Consultants, a relatively new institution that had been in Jalandhar for a little over two years, but that claimed to have sent over five thousand students to foreign universities in that period. There were other centres, some that had been around for over a decade, but Sukhpreet had heard good things about SAC. He was told by students from his college who had secured visas over the past year that SAC knew what it was doing.

'I have the application fee,' he said, and she finally looked up.

'You have to apply to four or five colleges if you want to improve your chances.'

'Yes, madam, I have the fee for three applications.'

She picked up the sheaf of papers he had placed before her and flipped through them. 'Diploma is best. Fastest to process, but you only get two years. After that, you have to manage.'

'Yes, that is fine,' he replied, feeling his palms start to sweat.

He had done his research and knew a diploma was his only option. A degree was out of the question, not only because the cost was prohibitive, but because he knew how poorly he had done in the IELTS. Most colleges insisted on a minimum score of 6 out of 10, but a degree required better grades as an undergraduate, which almost none of his classmates possessed. Colleges also asked for more paperwork, and a statement of purpose that would require him to pay another consultant. It was impossible, and he knew it. He could tell that Rita knew it, too, just by the way she looked at him. She finally picked up the papers and placed them in a binder, moving it to her right, atop a pile.

'Okay,' she said, 'I will create a profile for you. We can begin working on your application after you pay a processing fee. Come back with a receipt from the cashier and you will receive an email from our head office about your follow-up appointment. Bring your bank statement and proof of funds. The counsellor assigned to you will guide you through the next steps.'

'Thank you, madam,' he said, almost bowing before he stopped himself. It felt as if he had run a marathon, although this was just the first step. But he was in, one foot through the door, and all he had to do was keep moving, ticking one box after another, until he had that student visa stamped on his new passport. He could almost taste it, a subtle shift in the air, as if he had been placed in a capsule and separated from the tired, sweating hordes in the office.

He stepped out minutes later, blinking in the afternoon light, his eyes adjusting to the glare after a morning spent in the gloomy air-conditioned room. He looked for a small dhaba he could eat lunch in, wondering if it made more sense to head back to college for a cheaper meal. He was hungry, but also felt a lightness in the pit of his stomach. He had taken a decisive step towards his future, and would stop only when he landed in Brampton, in beautiful Canada.

It still felt unreal, the possibility of moving to a place where he could go boating in lakes that seemed impossibly blue in colour, or wrap himself in fur and look up as snowflakes landed gently on his tongue. It was a world at odds with the streets of Jalandhar, perennially blanketed with dust from passing automobiles, where every breath was marked with the sharp tang of petrol.

This was a fancier part of the city, which reassured him, because a counselling centre on one of the more rundown streets would not inspire confidence. The older institutes didn't charge high processing fees because they were paid by Canadian colleges for every successful application, but he hoped the payment to SAC would make them spend more time on him and increase the chances of his application being accepted. He could think about paying off his loans later.

Spotting a dhaba that looked less expensive than the restaurants alongside, he stepped inside. It was a simple place, and he was grateful, knowing the meal would be filling but affordable. He had to save as much as he could. Ordering a kulcha with dal, he thought about calling his mother, then decided to wait until he met the counsellor. He didn't want to raise her hopes. He would get all the facts, start the application process and then tell her what his chances of getting through were. After that, they could have a conversation about whom to approach for a temporary transfer of funds to inflate his bank account before applying for a visa.

Waiting for the food to arrive, he flipped out his phone. There were no messages from his cousin Dan on WhatsApp because it was long past midnight in Toronto. The messages would come by late evening when Dan awoke, before he headed out to his job. Sukhpreet didn't fully understand what his cousin did, but knew it had something to do with the delivery business. The company he worked for had given him a bicycle, and there were often photographs of Dan leaning against it, with some tall building in the background. Once, there were even a few photographs of him with a white woman, and Sukhpreet had zoomed in, marvelling at how a boy who had never spoken to a girl while growing up in Chukhiara had found the courage to stand next to a gori. It made him wonder if he would meet a white woman too. What if he fell in love with one and invited her home to meet his mother? How would she react? What would their neighbours say when he pulled up in a car with his gori girlfriend?

He was interrupted by a waiter, who placed a steel thali before him. Sukhpreet put away his phone and reached for the kulcha, tearing off a piece and dipping it into the dal.

He continued to think about Dan, and how his cousin had done what no one thought he could. A man without a real education and no work experience had managed to leave Punjab and start a new life in Canada. It made Sukhpreet feel superhuman; if his cousin could get out, nothing would stop him. It had been four years, and he missed Dan, but knew he could count on him when he arrived in Brampton himself.

'I'll take you to this club where women take their clothes off,' Dan had told him a few weeks ago, and Sukhpreet had almost shouted in shock. It had taken him hours to fall asleep that night. Toronto. It was such a strange word, but one he heard often in college, from classmates who had family or friends in the city. They all pronounced it differently, and he kept forgetting to ask Dan how the locals said it. Was it Turr-anto, Toe-run-toe, or Tarr-honn-toh? Maybe it didn't matter. Maybe they were free to call it what they wanted, after they were accepted and welcomed into Canada.

Finishing his meal, he paid and walked out of the dhaba, after checking to make sure he hadn't left any of his papers behind. They were all originals—his birth certificate, school leaving certificate, and HSC certificate declaring that he had scored 54 per cent. There was also a copy of the IELTS test he had given a few months ago. He had scored just 4.5, but knew he could do it two more times; he'd convince the counsellor that his score would improve. He would work on practice tests over the weekend now that SAC had accepted him as a candidate.

Making a list on the bus ride back to college, he considered what he would have to do over the coming weeks. The first thing was to finalize the diploma courses he could apply to and find out what each institution wanted as part of the application. He had all the papers, but wanted to check with the counsellor; he put it down as one of the things he needed to ask.

There was the big question mark around funds. They wanted him to bring a bank statement, which meant asking his uncle to transfer a certain amount as soon as possible. He had heard of students being asked for statements for six months, as opposed to three, and hoped that wouldn't happen. If it became a rule, it would mean asking for a loan now and applying six months later. There were other options, but he didn't want his mother to mortgage what was left of their fields. His uncle would not be happy, but Sukhpreet could convince him by offering a higher interest and faster repayment options. Dan had told him that earning in dollars meant being able to pay back any loan in a few years, and he would remember to mention that while speaking to his uncle. The thought of earning in dollars made him look out of the bus window, his mind drifting to what that first trip home would look like. Would he wear a suit? Rent a car from the airport?

Dan had not returned to Jalandhar, despite promising every year. He blamed it on work and how it was impossible to get time off because his company relied on him. Sukhpreet didn't mind. If he got to Canada, he hoped to spend time with his cousin and find stability. Work was important. It was only after their loans were repaid that they could breathe a little and take time off for a holiday.

As the bus approached his stop, he stood up and put away his pen and notebook. He looked forward to a nap in the hostel room he shared with two other students. They were usually out all day, roaming the streets on a motorcycle. The room would be empty, and he would be able to think about the day's events more carefully. He walked up the dark stairs and unlocked the door, putting away his papers before lying down. The room was musty despite an open window, and he wished the hostel would do something about the fans. They were impotent machines, swirling desultorily, their motors weak and on the verge of giving up. Some of his classmates rented rooms outside campus, or stayed with relatives, but this was his only option.

Thinking about his classmates reminded him of his mother. Maybe he should have called to let her know about the consultant, even if it was premature. He could picture her, sitting on the mud floor of their home, washing the plate she must have used for lunch, before lying down. He wished he could be with her, but knew that his presence here, in college, meant more. It sometimes felt as if his family was cursed, but it was wrong to think of circumstances that way. It was Waheguru alone who decided how their stories would turn out, and he mouthed a silent prayer by way of apology for questioning fate.

Closing his eyes, he thought about the past, and how little of it he could remember. Maybe it was because there was not much worth remembering. All he knew of his father was that he was kind and hardworking, a farmer who had left them two acres that would one day be used to pay for his ticket abroad. It was the thought of his older, and only, brother that upset him—a man he had grown up worshipping, now lost to them all, possibly lying in some unknown corner of their city, no longer in possession of his mind. Sukhpreet knew the fear that consumed his mother's waking hours, the thought that she could lose her younger boy to heroin, too, and there was nothing he could say to eliminate that worry, except for removing himself from the Punjab, and leaving for a land as foreign as the moon.

Sighing, he called her on WhatsApp, wondering if she had her mobile data turned on. She used it sparingly, afraid of crossing the limit imposed by Vodafone, and he wished she would do a video call, so he could show her the hostel, and perhaps walk around campus to help her see what it looked like. She always refused, insisting that she would look at him in the flesh when he returned home for Baisakhi. Until then, she said, it was something they should both practice for: their inevitable separation.

The sound of her voice brought him back to the present, and he sat up, greeting her.

'Sat Sri Akaal, Ma,' he said.

'Did you eat?' It was always her first question; one he knew she would ask for as long as she lived.

'Yes,' he said, then told her about the SAC, what it meant, and how long the process would take.

She said little, only asking about the country he was planning to move to, and where he would live. They skirted around the only question that mattered, about what it would cost and how they could convince the consular officer that he had enough to afford an education in Canada.

'I will stay with Dan,' he said, and she laughed.

'I don't know any Dan.'

'Ma, I meant Deepanshu.'

'I will never understand why he gave up that beautiful name for the goras.'

'They couldn't pronounce it, Ma. They don't understand our names or languages. He had to use something simpler. Dan is simple for them. They like it, and I think he likes it, too.'

'I hope you don't give up your name. You know what it means, and why your father chose it.'

'Yes, Ma, happiness, it means happiness. I can't just forget what my name means.'

'Not just happiness, it means inner joy,' she said, laughing again. 'It is a sense of peace only children of Waheguru are lucky enough to experience. Don't ever change it to San or Pan.'

They both laughed. Hanging up a few minutes later, he sat on the cot and reached for his bag, pulling out a notebook and drawing uneven lines on a blank page. He turned it and began listing questions he intended to ask Dan when they next spoke. Calling him Dan made him smile again, and he put aside the book, falling back on the cot. Would he have to change his name too, despite his mother's wishes? Neither of them had been on a plane, and everything his cousin had told him was about being prepared to change everything. How much would he have to give up, and how much of his identity would be erased to fit in? There were thousands like him, students in rooms across campuses, and in colleges across Jalandhar and Punjab, all prepared to do what Dan had done, and he thought about them, too. What would they all give up, and at what cost?

Pulling out his phone, he tapped the YouTube app, scrolling until he found a singer he liked. He didn't like the brash Punjabi hip-hop Dan kept sending him. It was fun at times but didn't move him the way devotional music always did. He found the song '*Chal Bandeya*' and pressed play. He would have had to use earphones if his roommates were in, and he shook his head at how everything they listened to was saturated in sounds from the West.

He had asked them about their musical preferences during his second week at college, eager to get them to listen to something he assumed would make them happy. They had laughed, calling him a farmer who would never forget his fields. It was meant to hurt him, but he liked their criticism, even if he was sad that the idea of being a farmer had been transformed into an insult by men who were here only because their fathers and grandfathers had tilled the land. It was as intrinsic to being Punjabi as the ideas of valour and sacrifice. He avoided his roommates from that point on, choosing to walk around the city, instead of spending weekends at impromptu parties in their room. He didn't touch alcohol and wondered at their insistence on breaking that fundamental religious tenet as casually as they did, smuggling in bottles of Old Monk with Pepsi, laughing as he politely refused them. He would return to the strong smell of cigarettes, his roommates asleep on the floor, his bed often taken over by strangers from other rooms. He would stifle the urge to shout, and find a corner to curl up in. His roommates never apologized. They just made him feel as if he were making things harder for everyone.

He knew they would want to know about SAC, where he intended to apply, and if he could help them with the IELTS. They had all visited SAC during the year, along with other agencies. Some had already paid immigration lawyers in Canada or the UK and were in the process of finding brokers who could create fraudulent documents and marksheets. They would stay up late, discussing the pros and cons of each country, or the ease with which a rule could be bent or broken. At times, when Sukhpreet passed shopfronts advertising tutors, visas or lawyers, he wondered if Punjab had always been this way, a land so beautiful, yet perennially condemned to send its young men away. It was probably why they returned like migratory birds, preening in bright colours, as if to remind themselves of what they had wilfully given up.

The thought ate into him often. Why was he to choose between Canada and Australia, never Calcutta and Assam? When did India become a land where Sikhs were not welcome, and was this an imagined slight on their part or based on a real fear of displacement? He had been raised on the same stories as his classmates, about Partition and Operation Blue Star, and days spent by ancestors on the run from British soldiers or Indian mobs. And yet, he struggled with the contradiction of how much pride the Indian flag could evoke when it fluttered briefly in the stands during a cricket match, or when the Olympic team walked out onto some sporting arena, holding it aloft before them.

A ping made him sit up and pause the music. It was WhatsApp, with a link to some video sent by his cousin, who must have risen at an unusual hour. He didn't feel like playing it, assuming it to be some new pop song about life in Brampton, but it turned out to be a video of men doing the bhangra. It had been shot on someone's phone, and the footage was blurry, as if the person filming it was dancing along, but it was clearly some foreign city and he saw the Canadian flag on a storefront.

'We're taking over Toronto,' Dan messaged, with a smiley emoji.

Sukhpreet sent a smiley in response, then paused the video. He didn't message his cousin, even though he wanted to ask what those men were doing. Why were they dancing in the middle of a street, and what did they hope to accomplish? Was it a message to people back home, that they had managed to stake some sort of claim? It confused him, the pride that this behaviour instilled in Dan, and his need to share it with Sukhpreet, as if it made him part of some revolution neither had signed up for, with no goals other than arrival and survival in a foreign country.

He knew he would have to listen to Dan talk about Brampton, and how he had managed to cheat a gora out of something or the other. He would have to laugh along, and it exhausted him because it made him feel as if these conversations were between two strangers, not between Sukhpreet and Deepanshu, who had grown up in the same village and sworn to grow old together. It felt as if they were now playacting, in roles chosen by people they would never know, part of some international pantomime featuring brown actors who would come home each year in flashy suits, with dollar bills in their pockets. There was a sense of artificiality about the whole thing, a false bravado and swagger that felt put on, and he dreaded taking his place in that long line of immigrants, becoming another version of a person his cousin had already turned into.

The phone was still in his hand as he lay down again. He placed it on the cot, then pushed it away. He needed a nap, but his roommates would be back by early evening. Sleep would have to wait until later. He considered sending Harneet a message, but decided not to. She would never respond after 4 p.m., and he knew little about what her life at home was like. All he knew was that he liked her, and that she probably liked him, too. Their friendship had grown slowly—one shared plate of aloo tikki at a time. She had recognized him when he turned up at Rainak Bazar a week after their first meeting. They had nodded at each other. She had allowed him to walk her to the bus, then had told him her name. Harneet Kaur. A name fit for a princess, he thought, conjuring her perfectly oval face and two pigtails that he longed to unpin. She was petite, but held herself straight, and he could sense a resolve few girls her age possessed.

It had become a quiet ritual in the weeks that followed, a respectful exchange of information about Jalandhar, what students spent their time doing, and what she thought of boys from colleges like his. It had taken him over a month and a half to ask about her own plans, and they had both been pleasantly surprised to uncover a shared hesitance about studying abroad.

He replayed that conversation, his eyes still closed. She had looked up as if for the first time when he mentioned not being convinced about a diploma in Canada. It felt as if he had tapped into something she had kept locked away until then, and he thought of it as the moment their friendship began. He asked for her number that evening and sent her a message the next day. They had begun to communicate more freely since, and he sometimes forwarded the videos Dan sent him, waiting for her to respond. It amazed him that someone like her could exist, a girl from Jalandhar who refused to accept that marrying and immigrating were the only options.

He told her about his family, how he had grown up without a father and had lost an older brother to drug abuse. She told him about her parents and the disappointment of their relatives because of her father's decision to live and work in Jalandhar. What they shared, he realized, was a sadness for something neither could define, a feeling of loss for an idea they couldn't articulate. It was as if they both knew they would eventually be forced to become people they were not, their lives at odds with what they expected the future to be like. He couldn't explain why he didn't want to leave, even though he knew there was no other plan. There was nothing for either of them here. He would graduate and struggle to find a job, while she would be forced to marry the first bachelor with a permanent residency card. Their paths were limited, but they wanted more, even as they knew their choices would be made by parents or relatives, and by what it meant to be from the Punjab.

She wouldn't respond, but he sent her Dan's latest video anyway, of the young men dancing. He knew she would find it funny, and that they could talk about it the following Friday. He wanted to tell her about SAC and ask for her help with the IELTS. She had done more practice tests than him and spoke English better than he did. She was, in general, better suited for everything and would get a student visa faster. The only advantage he had was time, because of the two years that lay between them. He wondered if she would consider applying to Canada, and if they would one day carry on their conversations under trees weighed down by snow, their hands in gloves as they grasped cups of coffee the way new immigrants did on Instagram. He thought of losing her to someone, or some country, and felt a hollowness within him. She was the only person he thought of as a friend in this city, and he would no longer have her the minute either of them went away.

He wanted to tell her how much he liked her, but couldn't imagine what she would say to that. He had never said those words to a girl before. He couldn't ask Dan for advice because he knew what his cousin thought of women. It was everywhere, this notion that men alone had the power to decide what women in their lives could do. Harneet was different because he felt as if her father was unlike most men he had known. He wished he could meet him, but it wouldn't happen. What would she introduce him as? Her friend? Girls weren't allowed to have male friends. He would be invited only if he scored that magical visa, and if he could somehow convince her to let him into her life. The thought frightened him with its specificity.

There was a shout outside his door before it opened. Both his roommates were back, and they had two friends with them. The room shrunk instantly. He wished, as he often did, for a place that was his alone, but couldn't afford one unless he found a part-time job. Then again, having a job would compel him to save, rather than spend on accommodation. The years that lay ahead called for sacrifice, for learning to do without, and putting his head down. Dan had been in

Canada for almost half a decade now but continued to work at all hours. That was the only way. It was a promise to anyone who left—work, and you may find some measure of success that allows you to sit back some day and finally take stock.

Nodding at his roommates, he walked to the door, ignoring their comments. It would be hours before their visitors left, and all he could hope for was an empty cot when he returned.

TORONTO

12 OCTOBER 2016

It was amusing how a ping could evoke hope or sadness in equal measure. Deepanshu Gill picked up his phone, his thumb readied by force of habit to accept the order without reading, then decided to check where the delivery was scheduled. It was harder to get orders than ever before. In the early days, less than three years ago, he had the luxury of picking where he wanted to go, while maintaining the minimum number of orders required by his app company. Now, requests for delivery would hang in the air for seconds before someone would accept. The new boys didn't care how far they had to cycle, only that the order was theirs for a delivery fee of $2.50.

By the time he was done checking out the address, the order had been accepted by a rider. It sometimes felt as if there were hundreds of them in parts of Mississauga that once had just three or four. He should have been promoted to the post of supervisor by now, but there had been no promotions announced for months. The company didn't need to, given how easy it was to recruit from an ever-expanding pool of international students. Deepanshu didn't want to resent them but found it hard not to. He knew they were just like him, young men mostly from the Punjab, trying to keep their heads above water. What angered him was their agreeability, the nonchalance with which they gave away their labour for a pittance, making it harder for everyone else in the process. He wanted to hold them each by the shoulders and ask them to refuse extra rides until they were paid more.

It was useless, of course. No one would refuse a ride because they all needed to earn as much as they could to pay off college fees. It was amusing how they rattled off diplomas they were supposedly studying for, in hospitality and biotechnology, human resources or catch-all courses in business management. He knew their stories the minute he saw them at an intersection, boxes of pizzas balanced precariously on bicycle carriers, waiting for the lights to turn. It was a path he had already walked down, although he had no diploma to show for it. It had taken him little over a year to figure out that the university he was to graduate from was just an office building churning out certificates as worthless as the paper they were printed on. The teachers were barely qualified, and the diplomas were ignored by recruiters. The college wanted fees, and the students wanted an excuse to stay in Canada, with a job that would transform student visas into permanent residency cards.

It was where the sadness came from, he thought—that this place they all assumed would lead them to safety, a card in their pockets declaring that they were legitimate; which they assumed they could live in and work from and raise families in, wasn't what it was meant to be. He no longer thought of that picture, of being a husband and father, because he no longer saw a way out of what he had willfully chosen. If a promotion did come, it would mean a few hundred dollars more, but that would change nothing about his circumstances. Where would he find a room, let alone an apartment or townhouse, for a wife and child? He thought of his first two years in Brampton, sharing a place with fourteen other students, ten on the same floor and four in the basement. It was unimaginable, the gap between what he had been shown in Chukhiara and what this had turned out to be.

There was another ping, and he decided to accept without checking. He had made three deliveries so far, and there were five hours to go before his shift ended. He needed between eleven and eighteen deliveries to earn what he needed. He had finally moved to a condominium with just three other roommates and had to pay his monthly share of $550. There were no savings in his account, but he had begun to send home $500 every month, and he knew what a difference that made to his parents. It was not enough for them to meet their monthly instalment on the mortgage, but it was a sign that their son had begun to earn. It was a promise, and a glimpse of opportunity. They had all sensed it, his parents and sisters, in the months before he left, when they would huddle around his phone. They would watch videos posted by men they had known, from villages around them, posing in front of big cars or holding up dollar bills. That was what they had wanted for him, too, foreign currency that would allow him to reach out and pull them up behind him.

Pushing the phone into his right trouser pocket, he climbed onto his bicycle and checked to see if the rear rack was fastened. Pedalling away towards the restaurant he was supposed to pick up the order from, he breathed in deeply and shivered. The leaves had begun to fall, and he would have to start dressing warmly within a couple of weeks. His bicycle would be almost useless by then, when snow would start to pile up, forcing him to step off and push at every corner. He imagined sweat pooling inside his winter coat, and the exhaustion that would start to build an hour into his shift. It was no use thinking about it now, but he couldn't stop himself. Winter stretched out into the distance, so he thought of green fields and the tips of tall grass flecked by the sun.

The restaurant was called Ali Baba, and he noticed multiple orders in plastic bags on a counter by the cashier as he walked in. A few other delivery employees stood in line, all brown men, but his was the only bicycle parked outside. When it was his turn, he picked up the order. It was a large one, packed into three bags, and he hoped the rack would hold them. Placing them one on top of the other was risky because Styrofoam boxes could be crushed, but he had no choice and sighed, anticipating a complaint logged minutes after his delivery. None of the day's orders had ended with a tip yet, and he didn't expect one with this either. It still surprised him, after all this time, the mean-spiritedness of people who could casually pay $100 for pizza and refuse a $5 tip. That surprise would curdle into anger in winter when he would feel his fingertips grow numb as he pushed his way through snow-covered walkways to ring the doorbells of townhouses. It felt as if the homes were mocking him—their well-lit interiors; the plumes of smoke rising from chimneys—as he would hand over a delivery and trudge back to his bicycle.

It was a two-kilometre ride to the drop-off point, which explained why the order had come to him instead of a car.

He thought about how app companies worked, and how computers could tell where an order was supposed to go. He thought about the people working at those companies too, how much they were paid, and how they would get bonuses and benefits that people like him, the ones doing the real work, would be denied. It had seemed like a gift when he first got the job, six months after arriving in Brampton. His friends had celebrated with pizza, congratulating him on his entry into the Canadian workplace. That euphoria had melted away within days, long before his first winter, as the idea of being condemned to ride a bicycle and deliver food right through the year began to take root. The longer he stayed, the harder it became to consider another job. He soon noticed that there were no options for him, or people like him, that every job opening required manual labour, or the crushing mindlessness of walking the corridors of a mall wearing a security jacket. All he could hope for, after a year and a half at the company, was the possibility of owning a car someday, with his role as delivery person essentially unchanged.

He hated how his mind would drag him down whenever he cycled towards a delivery. He hated how people he handed the food to almost never looked at him; how they sometimes mumbled their thanks and shut their doors, never acknowledging what it had taken for him to get there, to punch in codes at entrances to high-rise buildings, to take elevators to condominiums on fifteenth and twentieth floors, just one of many immigrants trapped like rats in a maze with no exit signs.

A car honked as it swept past, the shock prompting him to squeeze the brakes even though it was nowhere near his bicycle. He cursed at the driver in Punjabi, relishing the cuss words, his shout attracting passersby who stared before walking away. He cursed them, too, the goras who needed people like him but wanted to maintain the illusion that he didn't exist, that he was a statistic, not a man with dreams of his own. He had never seen a white delivery rider at his company. They could be as poor as he was but would always have options denied to him and others like him.

He had even considered working on his English for a while, and had downloaded the Duolingo app, practicing phrases for fifteen minutes every night, but it was an exercise in futility. He could never get the accent right, his tongue betraying him at every other syllable. He knew other Punjabis who had persevered, and managed in their own way to get into offices that never allowed him past the lobby. He sometimes thought of asking them how they had done it, how they had beaten the system, but knew they would say nothing. They looked down upon people like him, treating him as if he wasn't as hard working as they were, as if he had failed to do what they had done, and he resented them, too. It was like a taste of something sour always roiling at the pit of his stomach, and he couldn't recall if this was how he had felt back home, this emptiness that gnawed away incessantly.

Thinking of home was harder because he still had no idea when he would be able to make a trip. He had promised his parents he would visit within two years, but it had been four, and ticket prices had only risen. He would have to factor in the loss of income, the possibility of unpaid leave if he went away for more than a week. He was entitled to time off, but knew how precarious that could be, and how easily his manager could replace him with someone hungrier, or younger, or more desperate to boost the app rankings. At times, he felt as if losing the job alone could push him into trying something new, but there was always the fear of failing, of reliving what he had gone through in those early months in Canada, that prevented him from walking down that path of recklessness.

His delivery drop-off point was down a quiet street, and he looked at the townhouses, wondering how much they cost. It was an old habit, but he had begun to recognize the differences between expensive homes and ones that only looked as if they cost a lot. The price of a townhouse had shocked him when he first arrived, because he had been under the impression that anyone who moved to Canada could purchase a home with a patio and garden within a few years. He had spent hours on his phone in Jalandhar, looking at tours of mansions, imagining what his own would look like, and where his parents could be accommodated. That dream had died by his second year, when he saw how long it would take him to raise enough for a down payment. His minimum wage eliminated the possibility of a loan, and it had taken him a long time to forgive the Instagrammers who had made it all seem easy. He wondered if the homes they shared were even their own, or if they had been paid by real estate firms to make those videos. It made him feel foolish, like a villager he had always suspected he would be revealed to be.

Stopping in front of the townhouse marked for delivery, he made his way down a short walkway to the front door of a semi-detached home. Mississauga was once the borderlands, and he had heard of people buying detached townhouses for a hundred thousand dollars, a figure that seemed almost mythical considering what single-bedroom condominiums were now sold for. He liked the guessing game that involved sizing a person at the front door and gauging if they were immigrants, when they had arrived, and what they must have paid for the place they now occupied.

Ringing the doorbell, he kicked down his bicycle's stand and began removing the bags. The door opened and he saw a brown woman, not very young, but Indian. He nodded at her, but she didn't respond, reaching out a hand for the delivery. He couldn't tell if she was Punjabi, but knew she wouldn't tip him. He could predict when a customer would or wouldn't, by how happy they were to see him. If they were white, they almost always tipped, which amused him because of how much he blamed the goras for his condition. To him, it felt as if they were obligated to tip immigrant delivery boys to make up for the knowledge that they would never find themselves in those positions or allow their children to take those jobs.

When the door closed, he picked up his bicycle by the handlebars and wheeled it around, kicking back the stand and jumping on in one fluid motion. He cycled down the street, turning left onto the wider road, when his app beeped. He could guess what that meant if there was no tip forthcoming. The customer must have been upset about some delay or a missing item like a plastic fork. It could be anything. They could rate him for his demeanour, lack of enthusiasm, or whether he smiled while handing over the delivery. He, on the other hand, could neither say nor do anything. There was no way for him to blacklist a customer if he was abused, laughed at, or denied entry because someone had changed their mind about an order. He existed merely to pick up something and drop it, with no right to complain. It didn't even upset him as much as it used to, and he wondered if that meant he was finally giving up, or if he had accepted his place here as one of little value.

He began to hum a song, wondering where to park until the next order. It was just after 5 p.m., and he intended to head back to Brampton in four hours, which left him with enough time to pick up around seven more deliveries. It wouldn't be a great day, but he hoped to even things out over the weekend when chances of a tip were higher. Late-night deliveries paid best, but it had begun to feel as if people were not as nice as they used to be. Maybe his turban upset them. He had heard how the presence of more men from the Punjab had prompted anger outside Brampton, in Ontario's smaller cities. He had considered moving to Ottawa or Waterloo, but changed his mind after watching videos of lines outside McDonald's outlets, with students desperate for any job. He knew what that felt like and thanked Waheguru again, apologizing for the resentment he had felt just minutes ago. It was minimum wage, but he had a cot, and food, and he shared it with just three others, which was more than he could say for those who must have turned up over the past year. He thought of Sukhpreet, who would join him within months if things went according to plan. He would have to find him a place or ask his roommates to let him stay until they could both move to another place. He hoped they could do it within a year, but it could take much longer.

The question of whether Sukhpreet would make it sometimes kept him up at night. Moving would take a toll on his cousin, but there was no other way. They had all been raised to understand that to stay was to die, because to be young in the Punjab had always been a kind of death warrant. Those who gave it their all would get out, and what they did when they left mattered less than the act of escaping, because it meant having an opportunity to fight what fate would otherwise have in store. Those who stayed because they had no means of leaving, or because they had failed to find a way out, could only watch as their bodies and minds decayed, day by day, if they were lucky enough to find local employment, or escape the presence of heroin that haunted entire villages, decimating young and old without prejudice.

No, he was right to ask Sukhpreet to come, even if it meant his cousin would resent him when he found out what he had signed up for. All he could hope for was that moment of clarity when Sukhpreet would realize they were trapped, but in a prison of their own choosing. Maybe he, too, would come to treat it as a kind of freedom. Then again, who was to say he would end up like this, delivering food for a living? Who was to say he wouldn't rise to a position of authority, or become a businessman like so many other immigrants? Who was to say the Instagrammers were all lying?

His phone pinged again, and he accepted the order, wanting to end his shift and get home. He would be tired enough to fall asleep quickly, which was a blessing because staying awake made him think of his parents. He missed them and wouldn't be able to see them soon. They didn't ask him for more, but he was their only son, and his sisters had to be married. Their fields had shrunk to a third their size, the land given away in exchange for a plane ticket and fees for the first year of a diploma. It was the route Sukhpreet would take, too, built upon hope. An agent would create false documents, showing he could afford to pay for a two-year course. His cousin would arrive, start working, and hope to raise enough for a second year. If he failed, he would also drop out and use every dollar earned to pay an immigration lawyer.

At 8.45, he turned off notifications. A report of his deliveries would go to the company, and he would get an update to his digital wallet by the time he got home. He knew what the amount would be because it rarely fluctuated these days. There were rumours that riders would have to deduct another fee for the maintenance of their bicycles, and he wished they had legal advice. It would leave him with almost nothing at the end of every month, his vision of a visit home drifting further away, along with hopes of sending more money to his parents. Cycling towards Brampton, he heard Punjabi pop from more automobiles as he got nearer. Years ago, it would cheer him up. Now, it only made him despondent, the exuberance of the music at odds with his situation. He wanted to meet those studio magicians who churned out such catchy songs about a country that was so bleak. He could rattle off examples—from Manleen Rekhi's 'Brampton NYC' to Romey Maan's 'Brampton Jatti' and Babbu's 'Gaddi Red Challenger'—all about how amazing life could be for those who got that visa. Where was that life, he wanted to ask, and why were they not talking about what was real?

It was 10.30 by the time he got to the fourteen-storey building where he shared a condominium on the sixth floor. It was the only building on the street, the rest given over to townhouses, almost all housing students in their basements. Every owner was a millionaire, buying more homes and filling them with more students, their combined rent used to pay off each new mortgage. He would look down from his balcony upon those homes, and think of them as factories, churning out people and income, their wheels forever turning, making some people rich off the blood of a hundred others. It would never stop because supply was limitless. He knew, because he was still on that product line, his labour paying the salary of someone he would never meet, some faceless entity on the stock market becoming wealthier as he faded into insignificance.

Locking the bicycle to a steel bar outside the building, he waved his key fob at the buzzer and walked inside. If he was lucky, there would be leftovers. If not, he would have to cook. He had begun looking forward to Sukhpreet's arrival. Maybe they could have a fresh start in another part of this heartless city. It felt hopeless, but he was alive, and he had made it here, and that counted for something. Opening the door, he realized the place was empty. His roommates were still at work, or maybe they were done with their shifts and had decided to go out. They all had relatives in the area, but no close family members who could take them in. He was too exhausted to care.

The condominium was sparsely furnished, with two mattresses in the living room and two in the bedroom. His roommates in the living room had simpler ones, with duvets from Costco. The walls were bare, and the only other thing in his room was a portrait of Guru Nanak Dev Ji placed on a table and surrounded by four chairs, a set purchased from IKEA for $99 during an annual sale. Stepping into the kitchen, he saw two steel plates in the sink with remnants of that morning's meal and cursed. The building was old, and leftover food could attract cockroaches. They couldn't risk a visit from the superintendent because the lease had just two names on it. If the building decided to evict them, they would have to hire a lawyer, and his roommates hated lawyers as much as he did. They had all paid enough over the years to stay on after their visas had expired. An eviction before winter would be brutal in Brampton, where landlords were like kings, capable of charging whatever they wanted, sure of desperate student renters willing to pay.

He rolled up his sleeves and washed the dishes before opening the refrigerator. There were no fruits or vegetables, just sachets of ketchup and a vessel with leftover dal. The freezer had frozen paranthas, and he decided to have one with ketchup. He could go down to the local No Frills and pick up groceries in the morning. Placing an iron pan on the electric stove, he ripped open a packet of paranthas and placed one on the pan, adding a tablespoon of ghee. One of his roommates had mentioned that stores had begun locking away bottles of ghee and he wondered if it was a rumour. There were always students forced to steal to survive, but ghee thieves were new.

His phone rang and he walked to the living room, unzipping his rucksack. It was his mother, and he sat down before accepting the call. 'Sat Sri Akal, Ma,' he said, smiling.

He would have preferred a video call, but she rarely used her mobile data. He remembered Sukhpreet telling him this, too. He stopped himself from asking her to switch to video; she wouldn't do anything that hinted at a waste of money, and he knew better than to tell her he would send her more if the bill was high.

'Did you eat?' she asked, and he told her that he had. She would never understand the concept of frozen food.

'How is the job going?' she continued, and he spoke of his office, a place he had never visited. He told her about the computers there, and how his boss had asked him to consider doing a course that the company would pay for. He knew she wanted to ask if they had agreed to give him a raise, but she said nothing.

'They will promote me in a few months,' he said, and spoke of visiting them in the coming year. 'If Sukhpreet makes it here soon, we can save more and move into a bigger apartment. You and Babaji can come and stay for a few months when that happens.'

She didn't respond, and he wondered if this was because she had stopped believing anything he had to say. When had that happened, and how had he not noticed?

He rarely called his father, because they had long realized how little they had to say to each other. His father had given up on him, and maybe his mother had lowered her expectations as well but couldn't let go of the idea that her son would change their lives. Neither of them knew what he did for a living. All they saw was the paltry amount he transferred to their joint account each month. The principal on the mortgage had yet to be touched and wouldn't be unless he earned more than twice of what he was currently paid. He felt a tear threaten to trickle out from the corner of his left eye, and rubbed it, swallowing furiously as if willing himself to stay strong. His mother's voice always made him feel weak.

They spoke for a few more minutes, about nothing he could recall later. Promising to call over the weekend, he disconnected and continued to sit, staring at the room. Would this ever change, the sharing of tiny rooms with strangers, saving ten or twenty dollars each week? A part of him knew the answer, but he refused to say it out loud, as if doing so was like setting something in stone. There was a smell of something burning; he stood up and ran to the kitchen, reaching for the stove and turning down the temperature. Smoke poured in a steady stream from under the parantha. It was still brown on the top but had stuck to the bottom of the pan. When he flipped it, he exhaled at the charred underside, frustration overwhelming him. Carrying the pan to a dustbin near the stove, he pressed the opening lever down with his right foot and dropped the food in.

TORONTO

16 DECEMBER 2016

The problem with children was how they could get away with the worst possible behaviour, and you were always the problem if you dared to call it out. Maynard Wilson pressed the pillow on his head, hoping to drown out the sound. The thumping continued, echoing across the length of his ceiling, as the neighbour's children upstairs jumped across their bedroom. He had considered a formal letter of complaint, but it would accomplish nothing. The superintendent would laugh, before chucking it away. Maynard had always disliked the man. He was called Diego and had a surname that he couldn't pronounce and didn't bother to try. He knew Diego disliked him, too, but they kept their animosity in check, pretending to nod while crossing paths. So, that was not an option. Also, a letter deposited later meant little when the jumping was occurring now. The children did it every other day, before going to school and after getting back, as if they couldn't step into their condominium without announcing their presence with noise.

He sensed a movement by his bed and spotted Woody's wagging tail. Still holding the pillow, he stroked the dog's back with his foot. It was early for his breakfast, too, but he woke up whenever Maynard did. How many hours of sleep did a dog need as it grew older? Woody had been with him for seven years and was probably middle-aged in dog years.

Did dogs sleep less at that age, or more? Another thump from upstairs broke his train of thought, and he bit his lower lip in anger.

He thought of going up there and knocking on his neighbour's door, but that had failed before. It was a family from the Philippines, and the father had only shrugged apologetically the last time. 'They are kids, mister,' he had said, pointing to the two girls and a boy peeking out from behind him, staring at Maynard as if he were a villain in their story.

Why have three kids in a two-bedroom condominium, he had wondered. What was wrong with these people? They had lived there long before he moved in, and all three children had been raised in those two rooms. The eldest must have been around fourteen by now, which meant the couple had been there for a decade and a half. A part of him recoiled at the thought of growing up like they did, stuck in an apartment, with no idea of what a yard was like, or a patio. It made him think of his own childhood almost fondly. His parents didn't have much, but he and his sister had a huge backyard to play in, and access to a lake a few hundred metres away. It felt like paradise now. He thought of how his world had shrunk, moving from that light and space into smaller and smaller circles, as he left Orillia for Toronto, washing up at forty-nine into a single-bedroom condominium at 640 Rosebud Avenue.

The jumping ceased abruptly, but he held on to the pillow. It was a temporary reprieve. They must have been dragged to the dining table for breakfast, but there could still be a racket until they left for school. He breathed in deeply, grateful for the few hours of silence that would follow on a weekday. He wished they would just move away, but it would probably never happen. If they had lived here all this time and raised three children, a home of their own in the near future didn't seem likely. He guessed they were on minimum wage, the husband probably some kind of assistant at Shoppers Drug Mart, the wife working as a nurse or training to become one. It's why he resisted arguing with them, their accents always difficult to fathom, their inability to speak English restricting them to blue collar jobs they would inadvertently occupy until they retired.

Why have three children, he wondered again. Why have more than one child in a country where a burger and fries now cost almost $10? He couldn't even imagine going on a date, let alone becoming a parent. He had read about why immigrants did this; why they struggled all their lives and kept having children—in the hope that one of them would rise and pluck them all out of poverty. It was a gamble they bet everything on, though most were destined to fail. He didn't get it no matter how hard he tried. Cursing them under his breath, he kept his eyes closed. There was no question of going back to sleep, but a nap after lunch was still possible, and that would have to do.

Friday stretched out before him, the hours marked only by meals and minor chores. The bathtub needed scrubbing, and a bolt under the kitchen sink had to be tightened. There was nothing else to do—except for walks in the park with Woody. He wanted to take him to the vet for a check-up, but the rate had been hiked to $120 per consultation. It shocked him when he last called, arguing that a check-up barely lasted fifteen minutes. That was the fee, he was told. So, he hung up. It had been a year since the last examination, and Woody seemed okay, but he couldn't put off an appointment forever. He didn't want to think of how he would manage if the dog fell ill or had a condition that required hospitalization. Would he have to put him down? It was too much to bear. Putting him down would be expensive, too, he knew, stroking his dog's back, as a wave of guilt coursed through him. How could things be so difficult that a man couldn't take care of a dog anymore?

Woody stretched, compelling him to finally get out of bed. He had time for a shower, but it made more sense to walk the dog first. It would also calm him down, as a walk around the park opposite the building usually did. School would begin in forty-five minutes, and he wanted to get back before children began trooping in. Somehow, over the years, he had turned into someone who couldn't stand children anymore. It was not the case when he was younger, when he and his sister had imagined normal, boring lives with partners, nephews and nieces, and family barbecues on Thanksgiving. When did that dream die, and was it even their dream to begin with?

He didn't want to start the day feeling sorry for himself, but he couldn't help it. There was a sense of melancholy that dragged him down when he thought of his sister, and how they had drifted apart after their parents died. He didn't even know where she was. She had driven to British Columbia with a boyfriend almost a decade ago, the two of them choosing to live in a rented RV. It was her big adventure, and he had ridiculed her, warning that the life of a nomad was not what she thought it would be. It had made her furious that her younger brother, the college dropout working minimum wage at a Timmie's, could dare to comment on her choices.

Stepping off the bed, he shuffled to the bathroom and splashed his face with water, before brushing his teeth perfunctorily. Rinsing the brush, he placed it back in a chipped mug, and walked out, whistling for Woody. The dog barked, rushing to the front door, his tail wagging furiously. It always surprised Maynard, the joy an animal could experience from the smallest gestures. He wished he could feel the same way, that he could tell himself he was grateful for life, for being healthy and being able to walk, for a roof over his head even if there was just $275 in his bank account. But he couldn't. He couldn't remember the last time he felt anything close to gratitude. It was just a fog of bitterness and anxiety that enveloped him, settling upon his shoulders from the second he woke up, lifting briefly on evenings when he splurged on a six-pack of Molson. There was no point to anything, and hopelessness thickened the air around him for as far back as he could remember.

They stepped outside and walked down the stairs, Woody straining at the leash as Maynard tried to slow down. There was no one in the lobby. Diego would or wouldn't turn up at 9 a.m., even though he was supposed to be there. A little over a year ago, Maynard had emailed a complaint to the firm managing the building, asking them to hire a more competent superintendent. They hadn't replied, but he had begun to see Diego in the office more often after that letter. Things began to slide within a month though, and he suspected them of letting Diego know who had complained, which would explain why he barely glanced at Maynard from that point on. The superintendent lived on the premises too—a perk that allowed the office to hire managers for a pittance. All they had to offer was a rent-controlled condo, and they could get away with not giving employees a raise for years.

The driveway was empty as he and Woody walked to the end of the street, waiting for a green light before crossing to the park. It was the only advantage of living here, although it was one of the most sought-after neighbourhoods in Toronto. Forest Hill was where generational wealth settled, where innocuous driveways opened up to twelve-bedroom mansions with indoor pools. He could only sense that level of privilege when those gates sometimes opened, and he would spot luxury cars parked outside. He knew there must have been tremendous pushback from long-time residents when buildings began to rise in the locality, owned by property conglomerates eager for immigrants. The neighbours must have seethed at real estate prices dropping as temporary residents moved in, living like the Filipino family above him. He would have empathized if he was on the other side of those gates, but he wasn't, so he relished the anger his building must have engendered.

He walked into the park with Woody as schoolchildren began to arrive. There would be small, tight groups of them closer to 9 a.m., and he hoped Woody would go about his business and finish. He hated being around when the school bell rang, because they would all run past with voices raised, drowning him in a multitude of languages. None of the wealthier neighbours sent their children here, to the public elementary school. There were never more than three or four white faces, and he thought of the incongruity, how children whose families had lived in the area for generations now travelled to private schools many kilometres away to get away from newcomers who had usurped their territory. He thought of the word 'usurper', and how pleasant it sounded, belying the peril it implied.

He wasn't allowed to let Woody off the leash but did it anyway. There were no parents around yet, and he hated restraining his dog just because a few children felt anxious around pets. What sort of parents allowed their children to be afraid of dogs? Back in his day, pets could roam the streets and enter anyone's yard, without owners worrying about being reprimanded. Now, there were signs prohibiting dogs because of frightened children. He unhooked Woody's leash with gritted teeth, annoyed at how this made him feel like a trespasser.

The dog rushed into the bushes, and he waited. He was supposed to clean up after Woody, but rarely did, because it gave him a grim satisfaction not to. Let those snotty kids weep about dirtying their shoes, he thought every morning, pleased with that little victory. There were more children now, moving towards the school at the north end. He whistled for Woody and hooked the leash on, pulling him gently as he turned and walked back the way they had come. There were two women on the dirt path ahead, both large and both Black. One was pushing a baby's stroller, while the other walked a step behind, eating what looked like a burger. He saw something white fall and called out.

'You dropped something, ma'am,' he said, pointing.

The second woman looked down, then looked at him and sneered. As she bent to pick it up, he realized it was a paper napkin.

'Oh,' he said, 'I'm so sorry. I thought it was a handkerchief.'

'Sure you did,' she replied, turning away with the napkin and walking to a dustbin. They walked away without looking back, and he knew they were talking about him.

Why had he bothered? They must have thought he was just another racist white man telling them not to dirty his park, when all he wanted was to help them retrieve what he thought was a handkerchief. Why couldn't he mind his own business? He was furious all over again. He had to watch what he said, and think about everything before saying it, because everyone was out labelling Caucasians these days. The smallest of gestures could be misinterpreted, get referred to as microaggressions, and he knew the word because so many people on Reddit would trot it out every hour or so, attacking him for some perfectly reasonable post. The world had gone insane.

Woody veered off the path again, towards a bush, so he pulled the leash harder than he intended to, and was instantly mortified when he heard a yelp. He waited until the dog was closer, then reached down and patted him. He didn't want Woody to bear the brunt of his anger, but there was no one else. Deflated, he walked out of the park just as a group of children and their parents entered. He heard the languages, Mandarin and Punjabi, and others he couldn't recognize. Not a word of English.

It was amazing how Canada had changed within a few generations. What would his parents have said if he were to invite them and show them what this city was like? How would they react to a ride on the bus, surrounded by brown men pushing everyone around—their body odour permeating the seats—or shouting out to each other from one end of the vehicle to the other? If this was the great multicultural experience promised by the Liberals, his parents wouldn't want to be part of it. He didn't either, but he was stuck. There was no home to go back to in Orillia and, even if his parents hadn't sold it years ago, he didn't know if he could afford to maintain the place without a steady income. Taxes rose constantly, and his employment insurance was barely sufficient, only sustaining him because he had moved into the condo. If it weren't for rent control, he would be homeless. It was bleak.

Diego probably knew about his situation too, and it incensed him that someone who barely earned minimum wage could disparage him just because he survived on a government handout. It was a handout made possible by taxes that had been paid by his parents and grandparents, and people before them, and he sometimes wanted to scream this out not just to Diego but to the other residents who looked away when he walked into the lobby, as if he were some mascot for bad luck, a conduit for forces that could drag them down to his level of penury. I AM HERE BECAUSE OF PEOPLE LIKE YOU, he wanted to say; people who took jobs meant for those who had always lived here. Why didn't they all just go back to where they came from?

He was worked up now, breathing rapidly. It would take hours for the feeling to subside, and he wished he had somewhere to escape to. Even a job at Canadian Tire would be great, but he could no longer stomach the idea of working alongside men like his Filipino neighbour. Reaching the building, he swiped his key fob and pushed open the door forcefully. The lobby was still empty, and he glared at Diego's empty office. It was 9.15 a.m. and he should have been in, but wasn't, his absence an insult.

The apartment was quiet now, the children in school. He would have a bit of peace. Switching on his desktop computer, he made his breakfast of cereal and milk. There had been no blog updates for a few days, and he considered a post based on his interactions with the two Black women. He already had the perfect title: 'You're the One Trespassing in My Country but I'm the Asshole?' It was the right kind of what everyone online called 'clickbait', guaranteed to get votes when he uploaded it to Reddit. He looked forward to some immigrant bashing on the multiple groups he was part of. It made him feel as if he was fighting back in his own way, armed with nothing but a keyboard and a desire to take back his country from these coloured invaders.

There were hundreds like him now, across Canada, and he had begun to reach out to more of them. He thought of forming a new group, not as radical as America's Proud Boys, but something subtle, without the need for action in the real world. They could function as online ambassadors of some kind, infiltrating Liberal groups on Facebook and Reddit or other social media platforms that encouraged debate. That's what the newspapers were denying, after all, a platform for people to air their grievances. All he wanted was to talk about immigration. Everywhere he looked, there were Asians taking up jobs once reserved for working-class Canadians.

When he was done with breakfast, he logged onto Reddit and began writing:

> So these two women in the park think I'm racist just because I asked one of them to pick up something she dropped. This is what we get for doing the right thing for asking these people who don't belong here to clean up after their mess. This is what makes me the bad guy. And yes they don't belong here because these aren't the people we would meet in Ontario when I was growing up. It's not racist to say that if it's just a fact and when did facts become a problem around here?
>
> I didn't let her get away with it obviously, no way. I told her to pick up her trash and get out of the park. She looked at me like I was the devil and I could sense what she was thinking. How dare this white guy talk to me like this she must have thought and her companion staring too as if I was the one responsible for dirtying a public park.
>
> It's happening everywhere but no one wants to see it. Look at the filth in our parks and ask yourself if they were as dirty when you went to school. Look at our shopping centres and malls and ask yourself if it was so difficult to park your damn car when your parents went shopping. Take the TTC and count the number of white faces. They're taking over everything and we're welcoming them with open arms because the liberals think it makes Canada stronger. Speak up before it's too late.

> All I did was ask two coloured women to clean up and if that makes me a bad guy then I can live with that. What do you think patriots? Should we just lie down and let them walk all over us? Until next time this is the Weekend Warrior signing out. Stay strong and stay safe.

He read it once more before clicking the 'Post' button. It felt satisfying, like a drug being injected into his veins in small doses. He was doing *something* with his life. He would wait for an hour, then post it to other communities, and watch the comments roll in. So what if he was unemployed, and survived on government benefits? This was his way of contributing to society, and he was proud of it.

'Service to society is still work as far as I'm concerned,' he muttered to himself. 'They should be paying me a damn wage just for fighting on their behalf.'

Returning to the kitchen, he filled his electric kettle with water, before dropping a teabag into a mug. Pouring the boiling water in, he went back to his computer and clicked the refresh button. There were no comments, and he wondered if this was because he hadn't been posting as regularly as he ought to have. There was so much to write about, and he felt guilty about wasting time on YouTube. He began reading what he had written, saying the words out loud, imagining himself addressing an audience. He should have considered politics. His speeches would get a lot of people to rise up and change things, of this he was certain.

On a whim, he logged onto a site with job listings. It would infuriate him, but it was also a necessary exercise, the anger driving him to be more prolific as a blogger. He had one year of college on his resume, and wondered if he could lie on his CV and make it seem as if he had acquired a bachelor's degree. As long as no one asked for proof, it couldn't hurt. But what would it qualify him for? The listings all asked for experienced STEM professionals, and even employees at co-ops were required to have tech degrees from half-decent universities. How could they afford such qualifications? He had to drop out after a year, when his savings ran out, and he still had around $4,000 left to repay his student loan for a liberal arts degree. How was anyone supposed to become a well-qualified intern, let alone get a permanent, full-time job, when the only people who could afford the university fee structure were international students turning up with their parents' money? He typed in words like 'assistant' and 'trainee' and 'helper', but only found jobs related to healthcare. It was enough to make a regular person go insane.

Shutting the job site, he checked Reddit again, scrolling through communities he was part of, casually reading posts on r/ImmigrationCanada and r/CanadaExpressEntry, and noting what he could respond to. Things could get heated on those forums, but he looked forward to it. It was like a dance, the ability to say something offensive with just the right amount of vitriol, but not in a manner that could get you kicked out by a touchy moderator. You had to tread carefully, backing anything provocative with what appeared to be factual, because those were the posts that got more votes, slowly rising to the top of every debate. He had begun to make a name for himself in smaller communities from

Kitchener and Ottawa, and loved joining groups meant for students, because they were the easiest to bait.

Someone had put up a post about students and body odour, and he responded gleefully: 'Only animals who aren't familiar with civilized societies can walk around oblivious to BO.'

The post was flagged almost immediately, with a comment: 'You cannot refer to students as animals, and separating civilized societies from uncivilized ones is arrogance that borders on racism.'

Maynard clicked reply with a half-smile on his face: 'This is gaslighting on your part. I am referring to the need for civil behaviour because that is what we need for society to function effectively. You are turning this into a comment about racism. This is precisely what is going wrong with our country. No one can point fingers, no one can call out bad behaviour, and no one can say that what students are doing is right or wrong ... only because they happen to be foreigners. We must all bend over backwards and welcome them into our provinces and universities and homes because our government has put out a welcome mat without bothering to check their credentials or check with us. And I'm the bad guy because I suggest that putting on a little deodorant is a kind gesture.'

There were quick reactions, and he noted the number of votes. This was how you took your space back, he thought, one argument at a time.

The person who had posted the original comment responded after a few minutes: 'To turn around and call this gaslighting is what members of the Conservative party do when they have no valid arguments. You said something offensive and, instead of apologizing, turned that vile remark into an attack on liberal policies and immigration. Why don't you get off your high horse and accept that immigration, like all policies, has pros and cons? Why not use common sense to acknowledge that every policy is open to abuse? Why not consider facts for a change, and look at what good immigrants do for this country and its economy, instead of laying into those who supposedly exploit the system? I'd bet a week's pay that people like you who badmouth immigrants every chance you get are probably bitter because they do your job better than you, and you just can't stomach it.'

Maynard almost slammed the desk in anger. He loved this sort of argument, but wanted to calm down before responding with his first instinct, which was to abuse. Taking a deep breath, he began to type, reading his response aloud before posting: 'So many words for a comment with no substance. You automatically assume that everyone who doesn't agree with you is an angry Caucasian and then call them racist? If you can't come up with anything to back your claims, go and complete the useless degree you're probably working towards before posting garbage here.'

It wasn't a great response, but it would be enough to buy himself some time and support from others on the forum. The poster responded: 'It's obvious I'm dealing with a troll. No one said anything about you being Caucasian. This post was about body odour, and you have made it about immigration to suit yourself. I won't be drawn into your hateful agenda. Have a good life, loser.'

He laughed. To end a post with 'loser' meant that he had won. He had ruined the other person's composure and come out looking like the rational one. There were more votes for his responses, and he bent down to scratch Woody's head. 'That's how you do it,' he said. He thought of putting up a link to his recent blog in the same forum, now that he had attracted a bit of attention, but decided to try another group instead. There was no point arguing with the same bunch.

In his calmer moments, Maynard knew that there was nothing he could do to stop the immigrants who were already in, but he believed the warnings he posted could act as a deterrent for other brown and Black men or women thinking about making the move to his country. Enough was enough. Canada was full.

An hour crept by, and he made himself a sandwich for lunch while watching YouTube. He wanted a nap before school ended at 3 p.m. That familiar anger was starting to creep up on him again as he thought of being forced to live according to when his neighbour's children were home. He hated everything about this building, but there was nowhere else to go. He imagined himself on the same chair a few years from now, staring at his computer while eating a sandwich. This was what life had been reduced to: the loneliness of middle-age, with nothing to look forward to but a cheque from the government that barely covered rent. Breathing out slowly, he shut down his computer.

JALANDHAR

9 APRIL 2017

The line stretched around the building, spilling into an adjacent lane. Harneet continued to pray silently as she took her place. It was 8.30 a.m., and she had misjudged how early she should have come. Then again, it didn't matter because of how quickly things would move once the British Council office opened at 9 a.m. Results would be handed out within minutes. Passersby looked at the line and walked on, unconcerned. They were used to students on this street because the IELTS was held three to four times a month. There were other centres and institutions offering the test, but her father had always insisted on the British Council.

A girl in front turned around and smiled, looking at Harneet as if to gauge how well she could score.

'First time?' she asked, and Harneet nodded.

'Don't worry if it's not good. It takes two or three attempts to get more than 6.'

'Is this your second time?' Harneet asked, even though she didn't feel like a conversation.

'Third,' the girl said, smiling again. 'This time, I will get a 6.5.'

Harneet nodded, looking away. She was glad the girl had no more questions. They were all predictable, the conversations around what a score meant, how one could get better, or what universities were open to those who didn't get more than 5.5. She had heard of a student in Amritsar getting an 8 and had wondered if such a thing was possible. No one she knew had scored even a 7. The higher the score, the wider her prospects. She could then aim for a course or diploma she was genuinely interested in, as opposed to choosing something generic like human resources. What she liked studying was an unspoken question lying heavily on her tongue, bothering her ever since she had joined college. She would graduate with a bachelor's degree in sociology but was no closer to an answer.

The line began to move suddenly, as if someone had pulled a thread at one end. She saw students beginning to shift as they made their way to the building where the office was located. She thought of messaging Sukhpreet, but his phone would be on silent mode until his lectures ended at noon. She wished she could hear his voice; they had spoken the evening before, and he had promised to call after class. Speaking to him calmed her. It wasn't what he said as much as how he said it, with a quiet certainty that things would happen the way he said they would. She smiled thinking of the way they had met, and how neither could have foreseen this blossoming of friendship, circling around the edges of something deeper. Neither had spoken of it, as if afraid to break something fragile, and she wished she had the courage to tell him how she felt.

Students had begun to appear with envelopes in their hands, some clutching their results without looking at them, others speaking loudly on phones, and everyone in the line could sense how well the test had gone by looking at the faces of those who walked past. There was relief or indifference, but no joy. Or maybe the ones who were happy needed time to process what they had scored, acknowledging that they had taken one large step in a line of many hurdles still standing before them. It was exhausting to think about, and she remembered what Sukhpreet had said the day before. Look at the day, he said, not the month or year to come. All she had to do was collect her result and see whether it was enough. She could worry over colleges, diplomas, application fees and statements of purpose later. It was good advice, but she struggled to follow it.

She was close to the main street now, around 50 feet from the building. Her stomach felt queasy as she thought of the examination again, and the three gruelling hours it had taken. Why did it have to be so difficult, and why did they insist on English when no college in India asked students if they could read or write in any language before letting them in? She knew it was a ridiculous question, but it annoyed her nonetheless, more when she saw how hard Sukhpreet had worked to score enough for an application. The result was valid for just two years. He had tried repeatedly, but the score was what it was, and seats were hard to find. She knew he was desperate, and would have to take whatever he found, even if it meant studying something he had no inclination for. All that mattered was a letter of acceptance, so he could apply for a visa. She knew what it meant to his mother, but it left her with a deep sadness because she would lose him within months. They had no claim on each other, so why did this bother her?

The building was close, and she rummaged through her rucksack for the letter inviting her to pick up her results. As she climbed the stairs, waiting on each step for what felt like an eternity, she wondered how her parents would react if she didn't do well. Neither of them would say anything harsh because they both knew how hard she had worked. It would bother them though, because it would mean more classes, another application fee, and the stress of sitting through this process again. It took a toll on all of them, and she prayed to Waheguru that they wouldn't have to repeat it.

When it was her turn to go through the office doors, she saw that there was one more line to get past. A clerk looked at every letter, cross-checking the applicant's details and scrutinizing their proof of identity before handing over sealed envelopes. Some students didn't wait, ripping their envelopes open as they turned to the exit. Others placed the envelopes in their bags and walked away quietly, as if afraid of looking until they had found a safe space. Harneet decided to wait until she got home. Her mother would be there, and they could check the results together. She took a deep breath and held it, counting to thirty before exhaling. It was something her father had taught her when she was little, how breathing could affect the way she approached a problem. He loved learning about breathing techniques, and tried to get her to join him on weekends, when he would sit cross-legged on a straw mat and meditate, inhaling and exhaling while she and her mother watched television.

The girl before her got her envelope and walked away. Harneet looked after her for a second, wanting to wish her luck, but she didn't look back. The clerk sat behind the counter, her eyes on a computer screen. 'Next,' she said, and Harneet handed her the letter along with her college identification card. 'Passport?' the clerk asked, and Harneet handed it over. The clerk looked at the document carefully, and then at her. Satisfied, she rummaged through a sheaf of envelopes on a plastic tray and picked up one with her name on it.

Harneet thanked her, placing it in her handbag along with her passport. She zipped it up and turned away, then stopped before the exit to check that her name was on the envelope. She didn't want to get home and find someone else's results. Removing the envelope, she read the name again. It was hers, and what it contained would define what the rest of her year would look like. If she scored enough, she could begin her applications. If she didn't, it meant waiting for the next examination, and missing out on the year's intake. Her friends had told her of consultants who could get her seats even later. But it was impossible to know whom to trust—which was why she wanted to do things the right way, by applying to a college on her own, which meant having the right paperwork.

Walking out, she noticed how the line of students stayed the same, disappearing around the edge of the building to the street she had been on just a half hour ago. Results could be collected between 9 a.m. and the afternoon, and she thought of how many students would walk through those doors within three hours. They had all sat through the test and would do it again until they had a score that met with the approval of some foreign clerk on the other side of the planet. They would be evaluated and debated over; their worth judged by people interested mostly in their ability to pay a fee. She had cousins who had lived in England for four years but still couldn't speak English. Why did colleges insist on the IELTS when they knew most students were only interested in a visa?

She felt the metaphorical weight of the envelope, a simple sheet of paper telling her what she had scored in four sections: listening, reading, writing and speaking. That combined number meant admission to a real college or a fake one. There were more of them cropping up, institutions with names like Ajax School and A1 Institute, all offering programmes in subjects that meant nothing, and she had friends who applied to them too, willing to take the risk of turning up at an address that didn't exist, just so they could leave Jalandhar behind.

The ride home took a little over twenty minutes, and she closed her eyes. It hit her then—the hours of tuitions, practice tests, listening to BBC news readers pronounce words she would never use, preparing for questions about her life, her home and parents, while always being at the mercy of an examiner who could ask her to speak about politics in America to make sure she could communicate. But she had done it once and would do it again, if necessary, the way Sukhpreet had. She pulled out her phone and messaged, asking him to text her after class, even though she knew he would. They had discussed the possibility of a low score, and he had dismissed it, his confidence at odds with how little she trusted her own abilities.

Her mother was cooking when she walked through the door. She ran out of the kitchen when she heard Harneet and looked at her daughter's face carefully, trying to gauge what had happened. Harneet handed over the envelope and sat on a chair by the dining table. 'I haven't looked yet. Let's look together.'

Her mother stared at the envelope, then placed it on the table. 'No, let's eat first.'

'It's early for lunch. Should we wait for Papa?'

'Why wait until evening? We can look after lunch and see what he has to say based on your result.'

Harneet nodded, tired, although it was only a little past 10.30 a.m. She hadn't slept well, thinking about the results. It felt all too dramatic, this heaviness in her bones—the weight of her family's expectations. She had no idea how long the weight had lain on her shoulders, or for how many years, but it must have been part of her all along, probably from the day she was born, a girl child in the Punjab.

Her mother had returned to the kitchen, and the sound of something sizzling saddened Harneet. She saw an older version of herself, homemaker or wife or mother. She imagined what it would be like to write a role for herself. Would she ever know who she was, as a person, and as a woman, and would she be able to act upon that knowledge in the rare instance of it being made known to her? She felt as if she couldn't even articulate these questions. All she could do was grasp at the idea, hovering dimly in her consciousness, during those rare moments when examinations, student visas and applications receded.

Her mother returned a few minutes later, with two plates in her hand. Placing one before Harneet, she sat down beside her and nodded towards the food. They ate in silence, each thinking about things they never spoke about. Harneet often wondered what her mother would have been like if she weren't here, in this home, with this husband and daughter to take care of. Would she have been like some of those women on television, working in Delhi or Bombay, earning as much or more than their partners? She couldn't picture it. Her mother was not unhappy, that much she knew, and her father loved them both. Maybe she was projecting her own dissatisfaction, her own refusal to conform, on to her mother. Who was she to question her choices?

'Did you add methi to this parantha?' Harneet asked, not because she wanted an answer, but because she wanted to stop thinking.

'You noticed,' her mother said, looking up and smiling. 'I will show you how to do this on Saturday. Soak the seeds for half an hour before adding them to the dough.'

Harneet smiled and nodded.

'You have so much to learn about cooking, and there is not much time. If you get your visa this year, there are so many other things to do.'

Harneet didn't respond. This was an ongoing conversation between her parents, about what needed to be done, and how she would acquire skills to feed and support herself, or how much they could afford to send her every month after she left. She wished they could stop talking about it, but it would go on until the day they found themselves at the airport; her parents holding her close, while she would try not to cry. It was a moment she sometimes rehearsed while lying in bed, preparing for years without the only two people she had ever loved.

She waited until her mother finished eating, then picked up their plates and walked to the kitchen, rolling up the sleeves of her kameez to do the washing. She could hear her mother humming an old film song. As she washed the dishes, then packed uneaten paranthas in a plastic box, Harneet thought about the envelope still on the table. They had ignored it, as if to glance would jinx the result. It made her smile at the power this test had; all it did was prove that someone could speak a language. What if the goras had to do a version of the IELTS in an Indian language to get into an Indian university? How would they navigate the complexities of Urdu or Tamil or Marathi? It amused her, this insistence on English thrust upon everyone who wanted to study in the West.

When she was done, she dried her hands on a small towel hanging on a hook behind the kitchen door, then walked out. 'Wash your hands and we can open the envelope,' she said, and her mother nodded. She returned a minute later, looking at the envelope as if it were a sacred relic. Harneet laughed and said, 'Let's just open it,' reaching for it and gently pulling the flap apart. It wasn't stuck tightly, and the paper gave easily. She removed the folded sheet and handed it to her mother. 'You tell me.'

Her mother shook her head. 'I can't read English that well. You do it.'

Harneet unfolded the sheet, looked at it, and placed it face down on the table. She broke into a smile and said, '6.5.' Her mother jumped up and clapped, pulling her daughter towards her and embracing her tightly. They both turned to the framed picture of Guru Nanak on the wall behind them and bowed, praying in silence for a few seconds. When Harneet looked up, she saw tears roll down her mother's face, her eyes still closed.

'Why are you crying?' she asked softly, 'This is a great result.'

Her mother continued to pray, then wiped her face with the back of her palm. 'I'm crying because this means you are on your way,' she said.

It was a moment they had welcomed and dreaded. Her father would feel the same way, and she wished she could go back to a time when neither of them knew what an IELTS exam was. A score of 6.5—it transformed her into a potential student at a good college, as well as a potential bride for some well-off family looking for a way of sending their son abroad.

They had spoken of it in the past, people broadcasting what their daughters had scored, and how it felt like an auction. She knew her parents would never do the same thing but was aware of how the examination could turn her into an object of interest in certain circles. She had overheard the conversations often enough, how agents sought to pair boys who scored badly with girls who did well. There were intricate levels of bartering involved, where a girl's family could agree to a marriage on the condition that the boy's family would pay for the college fees and the plane tickets. There were agents who could conduct marriages before or after girls received their letters of admission, and who presented a range of options for applying for spousal visas, all of which made Harneet feel more like a commodity than a person. She had a cousin who had accepted the barter, and wondered where she was now, and if she was okay. Once again, she felt like an animal, fattening itself as much as possible, only so it could satisfy those who would massacre it for their meal later.

Sitting down again, she looked at the result, imagining what her father would say. They had tiptoed around this conversation for months, hardly daring to imagine a score that didn't require her to take the test a second time. What did girls her age do when they weren't preparing to leave home? Was it only girls in the Punjab who were raised to follow this narrow path to a visa? That couldn't be possible. She didn't want to think about it because it angered her, and because she knew how easily that feeling could tip over into resentment towards her parents.

Rubbing her face with both hands, as if to erase the tiredness, she stood up and told her mother that she needed a walk. It was noon, and the heat would be unbearable, but there was a small park not far from their building, a green space shared by a few thousand residents. It would be empty at this hour, and she needed to be alone.

Grabbing a dupatta to wrap around her face, she walked out, hoping her neighbours weren't around. They probably knew about her test, because everyone knew what the young people in the building were up to. They would ask about her plans, where she intended to immigrate, or when she intended to marry, and she was expected to respond with grace and good humour. Walking down the stairs, she realized that the one good thing about leaving meant living in a place where no one cared about what you were doing. She had heard of people dying alone in foreign countries, their bodies lying undisturbed for days until their doors were kicked down. It was meant to sound ominous, but would it be so bad to be left alone? If it meant dying in silence, was that so horrible?

Sweat trickled down the back of her salwar almost immediately as she stepped out of the building. There was no one around, except for cars that went past slowly, trying to avoid potholes. After a few minutes, she felt herself relax, as if walking without purpose were anchoring. It made her feel keenly how little time she had for herself; how so much had to be turned over to constantly serve some larger purpose.

Approaching the park entrance, she walked past a few trees towards the centre, where a large water fountain usually cooled the surrounding area. The water had been turned off, but there was always a circle of grass fed by the mist, a band of green in an otherwise unremarkable patch of dirt. The only other person around was the caretaker, an old man who pruned flowers and chased away couples caught holding hands. He must have noticed her and left only because she was by herself. She wondered if his salary was paid by the residents' association, a group of retired men tasked with playing morality police, forever on the lookout for some imagined act of subversion.

Her phone pinged and she started in surprise by how happy it made her, this realization that Sukhpreet's class was over. She knew it was him because no one else messaged her. She sensed that he was more comfortable messaging than speaking, and she liked that about him, his need to think about what he wanted to say, and his shyness that prevented him from saying what was really on his mind. It made her feel like a teacher, tasked with coercing this young man to reveal more of himself. The ping compelled her to consider, again, what her feelings were, or what they had begun to turn into. He was a friend, but there was also an aura of reassurance that emanated from him, making her feel protected the way her father's presence had always done.

'What was the score?' read the text.

'6.5.'

He called almost immediately, and she laughed as his scream made her move the phone away from her ear. '6.5. Super. You're coming to Toronto with me.'

'Why Toronto? Just because you're going?'

'Yes, because I'm going, and because your score is going to make it easy for you to get into a good college, not the fake one I am going to.'

'You don't know if it's fake. Why imagine the worst about this college?'

'How can a college that doesn't even have a proper website be good? Have you looked at it?'

'Of course I looked at it. I checked on the day you told me about your offer letter.'

'So, apply to a better college, and I will see you there in a little over a year.'

'I don't know where my parents want me to go. Papa also said there was the University of Birmingham where …'

'What Birmingham? Why Birmingham? Your friend Sukhpreet is not in Birmingham, he is going to be in Toronto, so tell your papa that.'

'What do I tell him? That I want to go to Toronto because of my friend Sukhpreet?'

'What is wrong with that?'

'Do you think my papa will be happy that I am making a decision because of some boy I speak to? Do you know what he will do if he finds out I have been speaking to you?'

'If it's a good boy with an offer letter from Toronto, why will he have a problem?'

'It's not that ...' She stopped, suddenly shy.

'What is it?' he asked, with that unnerving ability to gauge her shift in mood.

'Nothing.'

'Okay, let's not talk about Toronto or Birmingham. We can talk about your plans when we meet at the bazar.'

'Yes, but I'm not thinking about where to apply. It's just ...'

'You're thinking about what you scored.'

'It's not just the surprise of scoring more than 6. I don't know if my parents will say anything about my future because of this.'

'What do you mean?'

'You know that girls who score well on the IELTS are just ...'

'Just what? More marriageable?'

'Yes,' she said, softly.

It was the first time she had expressed the thought aloud, or alluded to it based on what he had said so clearly. They both knew this result could change things, not just for her, but her parents, and she wanted to tell him that she would consider Toronto if he gave her a reason to. She wanted him to explain why he wanted her there, and why it mattered. Most of all, she wanted him to stay, because he would be gone in a few months, and she would be at that aloo tikki stall on her own, the way she used to be before she liked the idea of not being there alone.

'What's wrong?'

'Let's talk about something else.'

'Like what?'

'I don't know.'

'Tell me about your family.'

So, she told him about her mother, and why she felt upset thinking about what she would become. She wanted to ask about his family too, but he wouldn't give too much away, apart from what he had already told her. All she knew was that his father was dead, and that his mother worked to support him. There was an older brother he rarely mentioned, and asking about them made him quieter.

'Why are you going to Canada?'

'You know why. I have nothing here.'

'That is not what I mean. This is a big country. You say there is nothing here, in Punjab, but what about Bombay? Or Delhi or Chennai?'

'I will go where I can earn enough to stop my mother from working. I need dollars. I don't have the luxury of waiting for rupees because that can take years. I don't have years.'

She said nothing, and he sighed, telling her he would call the next morning. She had upset him. Putting the phone back into the pocket of her salwar, she decided to walk home. Sukhpreet was still on her mind, and she thought of how important he had become. She couldn't describe what it was, this awkward bond they shared, even though they both knew it was love.

JALANDHAR

16 JULY 2017

Always look the other person in the eye while speaking to them. Sukhpreet recalled his mother saying that a long time ago. He followed that rule whenever he could, but the agent refused to look up. His name was Brijesh Gupta, and the board outside his office maintained that he had been an immigration consultant for fifteen years. The room was dingy and not air-conditioned. There were two ceiling fans, only one of which worked, whirling in a desultory manner above the man's head. The firm was called Top Star, and was the one Deepanshu had used, which was why Sukhpreet found himself in the same chair his cousin had presumably occupied almost half a decade ago.

There were other students in the waiting area, some with parents, looking through folders that held bank statements and other papers. Sukhpreet had everything he thought he needed, but Brijesh didn't look convinced. He was a short, angry-looking man with a tendency to mumble, forcing Sukhpreet to lean forward to catch every other word. He was dressed in a checked shirt that had been carelessly ironed, and there was a large food stain near the corner of his pocket. Sukhpreet wondered if Brijesh's clothes reflected his confidence or his failure to become a more successful agent with a larger office. There were enough agents in Jalandhar, but most of them asked for a consultancy fee upfront, before looking through a student's papers. Brijesh had said nothing about a fee so far. He had Sukhpreet's papers before him and held up the offer letter, as if to gauge its authenticity.

He looked at the bank statements, and asked about the mortgage his mother was prepared to take.

'Not enough for a visa,' he said, looking up at Sukhpreet for a split second before turning away. 'Consulate may refuse.'

'Should I borrow some more? I can ask Deepanshu ...'

'No need. We can adjust. You need to show funds, and we can do that.'

'How?'

The agent didn't respond. He continued to look at the papers, Sukhpreet's certificates and a deed listing the area of his mother's farm. Sukhpreet waited for an explanation, but all he heard were grunts as Brijesh kept poring over the documents. Eventually, he stopped, collected them together roughly, and pushed them towards Sukhpreet.

'So,' he said, and leaned back against his chair, arms folded in front of him. He had a large stomach and surprisingly slim wrists. Sukhpreet looked straight ahead, trying again to meet his eyes, but the agent only looked down.

'We will need to make some documents for you.'

'What kind of documents?'

'Your funds are only enough for six or seven months. Your course is two years. See the problem?'

'But Deepanshu went with the same amount ...'

'Who told you that? Deepanshu?'

'Yes, I told him how much we can get from the bank, and he said it would be enough, which is why I came to you.'

'Deepanshu asked you to come to me because it would not be enough. If it was enough, why would you need me?'

'I still need someone to fill out the visa application papers and ...'

'Yes, yes, I know. I know why you need an agent, but what you really need is to convince the consulate that you can afford to stay, and that you will come back to Jalandhar after your course is completed in two years. Two separate things.'

'But I don't want to come back ...'

'I know. You're not paying attention. I don't care if you come back or marry some gori and stay there and raise a family of half-white-half-brown kids. My job is to prepare your application and get you a visa, and I am telling you it is not enough.'

'Okay, so what should I do?'

'We will create new papers. Bank statements will have to be made, and a letter offering funds from a guarantor. Also, the farmland deed will be changed. It will have to be bigger, with more land.'

'I don't understand. I don't have anyone to guarantee more funds. And how do I get a deed to say the farm is larger? That is the registration stamp of the Chukhiara tehsildar. We use that document to pay property tax. How will I ask the tehsildar to sign for a document saying it's a larger farm? He will ask us to pay more taxes.'

'Who said you had to get any documents? Why do you think you're sitting here? And who cares if this is a stamp of some tehsildar from whatever place you mentioned?'

'Chukhiara.'

'Who cares? Are you not listening? We will create the documents. All you have to do is present them at the consulate and answer questions at the embassy. Can you do that much, or do I have to do that interview for you?'

Sukhpreet shook his head, still trying to process what Brijesh was telling him. They went over what Brijesh would organize, and what it would cost. It felt like ordering a meal at a restaurant. Every item had a fixed cost, depending upon where it would come from and who would need to look the other way. He had known this was possible, but to see how seamless it all was, how easily 2 acres could be turned into 12, and how 5,00,000 could be transformed into 25,00,000 rupees suddenly allowed him to understand how Deepanshu had done what seemed so miraculous. It was how so many boys like him, from Chukhiara and the villages around it, had vanished, as if by sleight of hand, turning up on video calls from countries he had only seen on a map painted on a wall inside their local school.

When he left Brijesh's office, he had half of what he had in the bank that morning, with the remaining sum pledged in return for everything that would make his application more solid. It frightened him, leaving for another country with a far smaller amount of money than he hoped, but there was Deepanshu, and the will to make it, which was no small thing. He would manage even if it meant surviving on one meal a day. He would go to Canada, work as many hours as he could, pay off the mortgage, and then take his mother with him.

It sometimes felt as if he had been doing this for years, even though the actual work had only begun when he appeared for the IELTS. Still, it had taken almost two years when one considered the research, tutorials for the test, the selection process and the raising of funds. If Deepanshu hadn't done it, he wondered if he would have the strength. Even now, although he knew Brijesh would get his papers ready, there was the matter of going ahead with the mortgage, applying for a visa, getting through an interview with the Canadian consulate and completing it all before the first semester began. There was also the possibility of missing his first term and being forced to reapply, which would make the second interview for a visa much harder to get through.

He wanted to call Harneet and tell her what the agent had said. She would probably have none of these problems, not only because her higher IELTS score allowed her to apply to more reputable colleges, but also because her parents had been saving for years. He wouldn't be surprised if she didn't even need a loan for a two-year course. It sometimes bothered him when they met, as he would idly think of how her parents would react if they were to come across him. What would they say about their only daughter being friends with a boy who had no prospects, applying to an institution no one had heard of, to do a course that would prepare him for nothing? He knew she didn't think poorly of him, but wondered if she knew how he sometimes viewed their strange friendship. He wished he could be more direct, and tell her how he felt about her, which is why a visa was so critical. He would feel more confident if he could announce to her that he had a plan, a way out, and that she could join him. Their lives abroad wouldn't be controlled by their families. Canada wasn't just a ticket out; it was a path where none had existed, and it came with the promise not just of a better life, but of one that was worth living.

Harneet was probably in class, which is where he would have been too if it weren't for this appointment. He messaged Deepaanshu instead, asking him to call when he woke up. It must have been around 2 a.m. in Toronto, but his phone pinged almost immediately, followed by a call.

'Why are you up so late?'

'I worked late. What happened?'

'Just met your agent, Brijesh.'

'He will sort it out. Don't worry. Just pay him what he asks and don't bargain. He doesn't like bargaining. Let him do his job and you will get that visa.'

'Why didn't you tell me he had to fix your papers?'

'I still don't know how he got them. I kept worrying that someone would find out they were fake. I kept thinking I would be deported. If I had told you this, you would have been too afraid to walk into his office.'

'What makes you think I'm not afraid now?'

'Because you met him and you're speaking to me, and we are both proof that this can be done. You're going to come here and we're going to do big things.'

Sukhpreet laughed. Deepanshu's enthusiasm was always contagious. It reminded him of when they were little, and the trouble his cousin would get him into. Deepanshu had a knack of being able to talk him into anything, just because he was always so sure that something would work out.

'How's work? I thought you said offices in Canada don't make you work for more than eight hours.'

'I do other stuff.'

'What other stuff?'

'Just other stuff. I don't just stick to one job.'

'You've never actually told me what your job is.'

'I told you, it's the food business. I work in the logistics department now.'

'But what does that mean? Do you have to sit in an office and do paperwork? What does logistics department mean?'

'Come here and I will show you. If you're good, they will hire you too, and you can work with me. I can be your boss.'

Sukhpreet laughed again, then asked his cousin to get some sleep after promising to chat over the weekend. He was hungry but decided to get back to his room and put away his papers before heading to the canteen. His roommates were both in when he opened the door. They had begun to speak to him more, now that they knew he had begun applying to colleges. They intended to apply, too, but struggled with their IELTS scores. They would have to take the test again. He sometimes overheard their conversations with parents or relatives, late at night when they assumed he was asleep. They would talk about forgery and paying off agents to appear for them, and he marvelled at how easy it was for some people to do the things he had worked on for so long. Besides, how could someone appear for your examination and get away with it? He had mentioned it to Harneet, and they had both spent a half hour trying to work out what it would take to pull something like that off.

They didn't ask where he had been. They looked at their phones while he opened the cupboard allocated to him and put away the plastic bag with his papers. He locked it and walked out without a word. They had long stopped asking him to join them for meals outside, realizing that he had almost no money. He knew they weren't too well off because no one with money would agree to share a room with two other people, but he also knew they had funds at their disposal and suspected that one or both of them were selling things they weren't supposed to on campus.

There were always rumours about how stuff could be procured for the right price. It made him think of his brother, a proud man once destined for the armed forces—until he succumbed to that white powder in college and walked out of their lives into a wasteland of his own making. Sukhpreet no longer hated him, but knew the blind love he had while growing up would never return. When he thought of him now, it was with a dull ache, as if he were thinking of a stranger who had once lived with him. His mother would never feel what he did; for her, Sukhpreet's brother would always be the older son she loved unconditionally, even as he broke her heart.

Sukhpreet didn't like thinking about his brother because it was like peeling off a Band-Aid, revealing things he had worked hard to forget. Walking towards the canteen, he looked at the other students in the hope that they would spark some other thought, some other idea that would make him turn away from his past.

The canteen was full, as always, and he ordered a plate of parantha he would have to carry outside. Students often sat beneath a few trees or ate standing up. They weren't allowed to take the plates with them, so he sometimes carried a lunchbox, taking the food back to his room. He didn't want to today because eating with his roommates was not pleasant. After paying for the parantha with curd and dal, he walked towards where a student sitting under a tree had just finished. The spot was pleasant and reminded him of his childhood in the fields, on days when he and his brother would carry a meal out to their father. It happened only on weekends when they weren't in school, but he remembered enjoying those moments. Their mother would be there too, and the four of them would laugh about things he could no longer recall.

He ate slowly, chewing his parantha while continuing to think about his family. He had tried explaining it to Harneet when she complained about something her father had said. He attempted speaking about his household, but couldn't, because she would never understand his past. He knew things weren't easy for her, but there was also a bubble that protected her from life outside Jalandhar. For her, unemployment or drug abuse were abstract concepts, words used in essays submitted for college reports. She knew of their existence but would be forever sheltered from the brutal force they exerted on so many like him. He sensed it was wrong to assume that marrying someone and moving abroad was easy for women, but he also wondered what it would feel like to have a life so carefully marked out, a future so clear that one could close one's eyes and float towards a distant harbour, surrounded by children and a husband, and an existence free of struggle.

Finishing his meal, he returned his plate before heading to the washroom. He washed his hands, shaking them dry vigorously as he walked back to the hostel. He wanted a nap, but his mind felt crowded, with too many things jostling for attention. As he approached the hostel entrance, he turned left instead and walked out of college. It was late in the afternoon and hot, but still more appealing than going back to his room and lying down.

Trucks drove past in a long line, as he walked with no destination in mind. There were knots of men at most corners, some huddled in circles around motorcycles parked haphazardly, others leaning on each other's shoulders and staring at everyone who walked past. There were few women, and Sukhpreet heard the comments made about any girl who walked too close to the men. They were vulgar and saddened him because this was not what the men in his village would do. The comments reminded him of his roommates, who would watch pornography on their phones and talk about women. They would laugh and thrust the phones in front of him, slapping each other on their backs when he would get up and leave.

A yell made him turn, and he saw an older woman holding on to the wrist of a young girl while shouting at four or five boys standing under a lamp post. The woman was screaming about god and cursing the boys, while the girl tried to pull her away. Sukhpreet assumed it was a mother and daughter; he could guess what had occurred. He had seen it before, the impunity with which men thought they could say what they liked about women, unless they were accompanied by male family members. It felt like a sickness—this relentless push for aggression; this role-playing at being macho.

A small crowd had gathered, and he considered getting involved, but stayed back, aware of how his skinny frame would accomplish nothing in the face of such naked hostility.

He was ashamed of his helplessness. The older woman was now in the centre of the circle, still screaming at one of the boys. He looked away, then suddenly lifted his arm and slapped her, the sound loud and sharp. Sukhpreet heard what felt like a collective intake of breath, followed by a sudden rush as passersby tried to get in-between the boys and the women. The young girl was in tears. The woman held her right palm to her cheek, stunned into silence. She glanced up and her eyes met Sukhpreet's. He looked away, then walked back the way he had come.

He felt out of breath, as if he had been running. He had nothing to do with what had occurred, but felt as if his actions had fallen short of the standards he ought to have set for himself. It made no sense, and he walked faster, as if pushing himself would lead to some realization that eluded him. The road would take him back to college, and the room he had wanted to escape, and part of him felt resentful of the women, even though they had done nothing.

What was it about the men in Punjab and Delhi and Agra and other cities in this part of India? Why did they feel as if they had god-given rights to treat anyone weaker, poorer, or female, as an item to be owned or discarded?

It angered him because it brought back memories of mornings in Chukhiara, during the weeks and months after his father's passing. He could only see now, with distance and time, that the neighbours and relatives who poured into their home had done so not because they cared about his mother and her sons, but because they saw a woman with land and the possibility of owning both. How could he have been so blind? He cursed himself for his stupidity; for the fact that he had left his mother to fend for herself—his conscience quelled by this sham of an education. It made him want to cry, and he slowed down.

He spotted a small dhaba. Walking in, he ordered a lassi from the boy who worked as a waiter. The place wasn't full, but there were enough students occupying its five benches to make it noisy. Sukhpreet said a silent prayer while trying to ignore the noise. It was as if silence was forbidden to residents of this city, as if it was only an endless stream of words and sound that could keep at bay the hopelessness that threatened to swallow anyone who dared to sit still in Jalandhar. He wished he could summon up the enthusiasm with which most of his classmates attacked each day.

The lassi arrived—a cold, tall glass sweating with condensation. He held it gratefully to his forehead and continued to pray. After a few seconds, he imagined his heartbeat slowing down. He breathed in deeply and leaned back. The students around him laughed, hurling abuse at each other, some playing music on their phones. He wished he could lock himself in a dark corner, away from people. Pulling out his phone, he scrolled through messages sent by Deepanshu.

Neither he nor his cousin liked typing. Theirs was a dialogue marked by the one-sided exchange of videos and pictures, and he looked at them, places in Toronto he couldn't name, a stream of white women clicked surreptitiously by Deepanshu, and videos of Punjabi men doing the bhangra outside a mall or on the streets. He couldn't explain how it made him feel, to see them rolling their shoulders to music in places so far from the fields that had given birth to those movements. It made him want to call Deepanshu again, if only to know an assurance he didn't feel, that he too would be there soon. He imagined taking his mother to see those dancing boys, and the look on her face when she would walk past buildings that reached for a clearer, bluer sky.

He often suspected that Deepanshu was not telling him everything. He didn't know what kind of apartment his cousin lived in, or where he worked, and he had never explained why he couldn't visit Jalandhar, even though it had been years since he had left. There were vague reasons about leave, and the cost of tickets, and not being able to convince his boss, but it had begun to feel like a series of excuses. He knew Deepanshu missed his own parents, and they had loans to be repaid, but it felt as if his cousin swerved away from the real world. His conversations were always about the future, a bright place where he and Sukhpreet would own big cars and large mansions, and would drive through foreign streets playing bhangra-pop with the windows rolled down.

Finishing his lassi, Sukhpreet paid and walked out, his mind still occupied with Toronto. He was close, or as close as an offer letter from a Canadian college could get him, and knew he could convince the embassy that his intentions were genuine if the agent managed to get him the papers.

His phone rang as he walked past the college gates, and he smiled when he saw Harneet's name. He wanted to tell her what had happened with the mother and daughter, then decided not to because it would upset her, and because she had nothing to do with the men of this brutal city. She sounded happy and told him about colleges she had begun to consider. She knew he wanted her to choose Canada but added that her parents wanted her to apply to the UK as well. Neither of them mentioned application fees.

'Come to Toronto,' he said, stumbling over the city's name as he often did, sure he was pronouncing it incorrectly because Deepanshu couldn't speak much English.

'Yes, yes,' she replied. 'You keep asking me to come there, but never tell me why.'

'What do you mean why? Canada is great. And Toronto is a great city.'

'Yes, but it is not the only great city. Have you heard that song "Nachda Saara London"? I think it's by Herbie Sahara.'

'No, send me a link. But are you saying you're applying to London because you like the music?'

'I'm saying I will apply to Canada if you give me a good reason.'

He didn't respond, and she stayed silent as well, as if they were both trying to work up the courage to put aside this banter and talk about what they really wanted to.

'Harneet ...' he said, after a few seconds.

She didn't reply.

'Harneet, you know why I want you to choose Canada.'

'Because it's a great country with lots of good colleges?'

'Yes, but that's not why. I'm asking you to choose it because that's where I'm going.'

She didn't say anything for a while, and he looked at his phone to see if she was still on the call. When she spoke, her voice was softer, and he had to stop walking to catch what she was saying.

'Why do you want me to come there just because you're going?'

'You know why.'

'No, I don't.'

'Harneet …'

A group of boys from college walked past, singing a song loudly.

'I'm at college,' he said. 'We can chat later if you're free. I don't know if I can call from my room.'

'It's fine,' she said, 'I can call at this time tomorrow.'

There was more he wanted to say, but the moment had passed. Putting away his phone, he walked towards the hostel, thinking about what he should have told her. Less than an hour had passed since he had left his roommates, and there was nowhere to go. He climbed the stairs to his room slowly, thinking about how many more weeks he would have to wait before the visa came through. If the interview went well, he would have to buy a ticket and leave soon after graduating. He wouldn't be able to spend more than a few days with his mother. It sometimes felt like too much, too fast. Life would sweep him up and deposit him somewhere, and all he could hope for was courage and enough luck to help him land on his feet.

TORONTO

7 MARCH 2018

They were all foreigners, most of them carrying rucksacks, chatting loudly, a cacophony that made him turn down the volume on his computer. They were in line for jobs at a Tim Hortons somewhere in Mississauga, and Maynard's upper lip curled in distaste. International students were not allowed to work more than twenty hours a week, but no one followed the rule. There were more such videos these days, which meant there were more people recording, or that no one had paid much attention to this before.

He couldn't recall there being so many applicants during the years he worked downtown, but it was possible that he hadn't noticed, because no one cared about immigrants to this extent back then. They were always present, a faceless mass on the periphery, and he thought of how foolish he had been, and naïve, to assume that these people coming to Canada were bringing something good with them. Diversity, they said, his bosses and the Liberal politicians he voted for. He had believed them, this ridiculous idea of a melting pot where the best of humanity would gather to build something new and exciting. What an idiot he had been, and others like him, dulled into a false sense of security, while this beast lurking beneath their gaze grew stronger, swallowing them all.

Clicking the stop icon, he pushed back his chair and stepped away. Woody, dozing by his feet, looked up before closing his eyes again. Maynard bent down to scratch the dog's head, then walked to the kitchen for a glass of water. He didn't like watching those videos, but also felt as if he was shirking his duties if he didn't share them. How much longer were they supposed to take this? If Canadians couldn't get jobs at Timmie's anymore, what sort of future were they hurtling towards?

There was a knock at the door, which surprised him because he wasn't expecting anyone. When he opened it, there was an envelope on the floor, marked with the logo of the company that owned the building. He knew what that meant: a rental increase. The building was old and protected by the rent control act, so they couldn't increase it by more than $50 or $60. But, still, it added up; $50 could creep up to a thousand or two by the time he was in his late fifties. He was already paying almost $900 a month. New tenants in the building were being charged $1600 for the same space. Of course, he didn't care about their predicament. No one asked them to come, and he wouldn't glance at them twice if they were evicted. What frightened him was the amount he would have to pay in a few years. The rent was $750 when he had moved in. He almost laughed thinking about how unaffordable he thought that was at the time.

His life was so far from what he had envisioned as a young man when he had moved to Toronto, armed with the vitality that only twenty-somethings possess, confident that he would find a great job, meet someone, marry and raise a family in a cozy townhouse. He had pictured walks along Lake Ontario on weekends, and picnics at High Park, children pulling his hand and dragging him to see reindeer sitting forlornly in their enclosures. When did that picture fade away?

The door was still open, and he realized he had been staring at the wall across the passageway. Shutting it, he placed the unopened envelope beside his computer, and sat down, pressing play. The video had been taken by some Canadian trying to be a journalist, asking people in line what they were applying for and how long they had been waiting. Maybe he was a do-gooder, trying to draw attention to the immigrant's plight. Maynard couldn't understand the accents, but he guessed that the students spoke of waiting for four hours for an interview. How were they supposed to work a counter at Timmie's if they couldn't get through a whole sentence without fumbling? He swore, thinking of the summer he had spent at Canadian Tire, his minimum wage more than adequate for a studio apartment and some great weekends at the Dakota, an old bar he hoped was still around, even though he hadn't been to a pub since he had lost his last job.

'Those were the days, Woody,' he said out loud, his voice prompting the dog to open his eyes. He moved his tail as if considering whether to wag it. Maynard began copying links to more videos and posting them on Reddit groups dedicated to colleges across Ontario. They came with the guarantee of angry comments. The outrage was palpable, and made him feel less alone, as if there were others like him all doing their best to keep these foreigners at bay. When he was done, he scrolled through the day's debates, considering which ones to join.

'What happened to college?' read one, by someone with the username @KayShmay. It had already received 209 comments. He read the original post with satisfaction:

> I won't name my college, but it's ridiculous what's going on. Our instructor admitted that, years ago, his lectures were two hours long. Now they barely last fifty minutes and he says he had to make exams easier to pass. Why? So that international students with their poor English skills and general lack of interest in the program can pass. Almost every student in my class is an international student with plans of getting a post-graduate work permit. What does this do but devalue education for those of us who are genuinely interested in being there? People are starting to call our college a diploma mill. How did this happen? Why was this allowed? It's not like it's a private institution, it's publicly funded! Who benefits from this? I think it's fine to have international students attend our post-secondary institutions, but under no circumstances should we be lowering standards!

Most of the replies echoed what Maynard was thinking, and he kept clicking the like icon, boosting them for more visibility:

@alpinetime: 'It happened cause colleges realized they could take advantage of low-skilled immigrants wanting a quick way for permanent residency and basically charging them up the ass for it and popping them back out. It's 100% corporate greed. They are making a massive profit and do not care about the consequences.'

@ManOWar: 'A significant number of programs have literally NO Canadian applicants. If a program has such little value that not a single Canadian applies, why does it even exist?'

@Neckks: 'Colleges and our government love Indians. They will pay five times the price for tuition and have no problem working for minimum wage. Why hire Westerners who will just complain about bad pay when Indians will do it without hesitation?'

@DomoMajor: 'My friend moved here from India in 2016, he graduated from my college and now teaches there. He's paid peanuts and the hiring manager told him it didn't matter what he taught. He's 27 years old LOL.'

Maynard nodded. He clicked open Notepad and began drafting a response:

> This is what happens when Canadians don't get together to fight. This could have been avoided but we sat around and watched television instead. Some of you traitors voted with your fake conscience instead of common sense, which is why the bloody Liberals have been able to take us for a ride and bring in more immigrants than we know what to do with. Where are they going to live? More importantly where are your children going to live when they get out of college? There's still time if we send the right kind of message that this sort of thing won't fly anymore. And if this message requires violence I'm not afraid to say it. My grandfather fought for this country and died broke because of people like these students, coming in and

> sucking out everything that's great about our country. Just benefits scroungers the lot of them, refusing to work and stealing from the EI taken from taxes paid by the rest of us. Wake up before it's too late.

He read it out loud, making a few corrections before posting it. It was almost 2 p.m. He turned off his computer and decided to have lunch. 'That was a morning well spent, eh?' he said, looking down at Woody. Walking to the refrigerator, he pulled out a packet of tortillas, along with a block of cheddar cheese and a tomato. He also reached for a bag of Purina Dog Chow in the cabinet under the sink. It was almost empty, and he thought about his last trip to Walmart. Dog Chow used to cost $10 for a 14-kilogram pack, and now cost almost $25 without taxes. It was robbery, the way they hiked prices because they could. Were pets supposed to be some kind of luxury now?

Placing a bowl before Woody, he went back to the kitchen and picked up his tortilla, chewing as he walked across the room. It was bare, except for a bookshelf, table and chair. Everything had come from IKEA years ago, and he debated, idly, what it would take to make the place brighter and more inviting. He had never had a guest over, and didn't know whom to call, but he liked the idea of a more comfortable apartment. When he was done eating, he drank a glass of water and returned to his chair. Turning the computer back on, he looked at votes for his last post, along with comments under each video. There was also a red dot at the right of the screen, indicating a private message. It was from someone with the username @WhiteKnight: 'I've been reading a lot of your stuff and wanted to congratulate you because you're one of the few people on these damn community boards who isn't afraid to say what we're all thinking. Great work, man.'

Maynard read the message again, then sat back and laughed. He thought of replying to this stranger, then decided to wait. At last, proof that his work was being noticed. This was why he did what he did, because the time to be silent was over. He wanted more Canadians to be like him, to say what was on their minds without worrying about whether the world thought they were racist. 'Who cares?' he said out loud. 'Who bloody cares if you think I'm racist?'

There were more notifications popping up, but he didn't check them. It was easier to let the comments flow on their own and stir things around only if the energy started to flag. It looked as if the videos would generate comments without his help. There were a few other places he wanted to post them to, and he clicked open a document listing groups related to immigration that usually responded well to anything he uploaded. Posting on college groups was not always helpful because there were usually a few students who would request moderators to delete his comments.

As always, he thought about applying to a few part-time jobs. And again, he realized that they all asked for skills or work experience he didn't possess. A single-page resume with two years at Canadian Tire, a six-month cashier's job at Timmie's and six years at Walmart would not do. Everyone wanted trained workers in their stores, and white-collar jobs asked for computer skills, degrees or knowledge of things he had never heard about: SEO, digital marketing, customer journeys or change management. It frustrated him.

No ... he couldn't go back to a store. Anyway, Walmart would never take him back, and he was probably blacklisted by their HR managers. He didn't blame them because they had to pay his co-worker a significant amount of money for what Maynard had said. That was what angered him, that the Bangladeshi guy he had called an animal had walked away with $100,000. He was the one who should have sued the company for not promoting him, despite his experience. It was discrimination against white men—he was the one at home without a job for years, worried about paying rent. It was unfair and appalling.

He stood up angrily, thinking about taking a break. He knew this would happen the minute he began looking for jobs—this rising fury. It always did. But how much longer would he be able to manage without any money coming in? Employment insurance would soon fall short, given rent increases, and he didn't want to think about what grocery stores would charge for eggs, bread and dog food.

Woody had gone back to his spot by the chair, his empty bowl abandoned in the kitchen. Maynard picked it up and washed it, along with his plate, then wiped his hands. A walk would be good for him, but it was too hot, and school would end soon. There was a small window between when the children went home and when those who played in the evenings would return to the park. God, he hated them all. He hated having to put Woody on a leash. He remembered being much nicer, more social, until that nasty business at work had pushed him into this corner. It hadn't even been his fault. His co-worker had been there for four months, and he remembered being livid that they were both being paid the same amount. What sense did it make? All he had done was give the guy a push and call him a monkey because he hadn't stacked the toilet paper correctly. It was harmless, a little humour on the job. The foreigner had milked it, complaining to the supervisor, emailing a note about harassment, then enjoying paid time off, while Maynard had been suspended within days.

He shook his head, looking down at Woody who would never have to deal with this. Dogs really had it good, he thought, because they didn't need to contend with foreign dogs coming in and taking their place. There was always a warm home, and there was food. Human beings were the ones who needed taking care of, and that was the problem with this world.

Sitting down again, he decided to wait for an hour before walking to the park. He checked Reddit again, posted the videos of student job applicants to a few more groups, then decided to respond to questions on r/CanadaImmigration, where concerns about citizenship, visas and residency were supposed to be answered. He knew the moderators would kick him out if he said anything provocative, so he began posting links to statistics about unemployment in Canada, and the housing crisis.

A post on the group for Kitchener caught his eye. It was an article with the headline: 'Brampton Food Banks are Banning International Students from Using Their Services'. He scrolled through the comments. Someone called @UserFound2030 had written: 'This should be standard across Canada. I stopped donating when I saw instructional videos for foreign students. I'm sure I'm not the only one.

These services are for Canadians that are struggling, not students who faked their finances to gain entry.'

He googled: 'youtube international students canada food bank' and clicked on the first video. It had a student, a brown guy, speaking in what he assumed was Hindi or Punjabi, and the glee on his face was obvious. He held up two plastic bags of groceries and did a little dance, the signboard for a food bank displayed prominently behind him. There were more students like him, all men. Maynard stopped the video and clicked on another one. There were more than twenty videos, and he checked each for a few seconds, as if to confirm that they all involved food banks and immigrants. He swore again before closing the browser window. Then, a few seconds later, he opened a new window and googled: 'Brampton scams'.

The hour passed quickly as he looked at articles, copying and pasting information into a notepad, typing furiously as he listed points for future posts. There was a lot, and he cracked his knuckles now and again, sticking his tongue out the way he always did while concentrating. Just as he decided to shut down the computer and take Woody for a walk, his phone pinged. It was an email notification and he logged on to Gmail. It was a message from the Canada Revenue Agency about a cyberattack, informing him that its online services would be temporarily shut down. This meant that anyone attempting to apply for benefits would be unable to do so until further notice.

He slammed the table with his fist, surprising Woody, who woke up and began to bark. 'Shut up,' he said, reading the email again, then checking the date. His EI payment was due in a week, and he had no idea how long it took for anyone to recover from a cyberattack. He didn't even know what it meant. Was his bank account safe? Was he supposed to change passwords? Standing up in anger, he walked to the bedroom where Woody's leash hung. 'Let's go,' he said, and the dog jumped up.

He walked down the stairs, passing the office without looking to see if Diego was in. He wanted to tell him about his kitchen faucet, which was loose, but didn't feel like having a conversation. Diego could probably tell that Maynard survived on employment benefits. As building superintendent, he knew what every tenant paid as rent, and knew that those who didn't move out within a couple of years didn't have the money to leave. There weren't too many Caucasians left, except for an old woman rumoured to be almost a hundred years old, who had been living there for three decades. Maynard had never met her and wondered how she managed. There were homes for seniors in the locality, but their rents were ridiculous, so he sympathized with her. It sometimes kept him up at night, the possibility of ending up like that, an old white man with no family or friends, trying to keep up with rent and groceries on a budget that shrank each year.

Entering the park, he walked towards a bench and sat down. It was still hot, and most of the children had left. There were a few stragglers, but they were some distance away. As Woody sniffed around the bench and tugged at his leash, Maynard looked up at the trees, their leaves swaying, the sky behind them a deep, shocking blue—the kind that only existed in North America. He needed a job and couldn't put it off for much longer. He thought about his sister again. Maybe she was married with children, or stuck like he was, with no prospects and the looming shock of middle-aged hopelessness bearing down upon her. Maybe they could have had a chance if they had stuck together, saving their home from being sold, and finding a way of making it. But speculation was a waste of time.

Standing up slowly, he felt his right knee hurt a little. It was as if his body had begun sending him signals too. What if he needed a knee replacement at fifty, or surgery if he slipped and fell on the ice during a dark winter? It made him want to stay indoors as much as he could, and he couldn't reconcile that notion with the years spent outdoors as a child, swimming or camping in the woods, climbing up trees without fear of falling. Where had that nonchalance gone, that belief in immortality? Poverty was cruel in all kinds of ways, but cruellest when it prevented one from enjoying what everyone else could take for granted, like a jog through a ravine or a swim in Lake Simcoe. Apparently, most lakes in Ontario were no longer safe for swimmers, and he shook his head sadly. At least the world was going to hell with him, which was some consolation.

He began walking slowly, with Woody stopping every few feet. Things couldn't go on like this, and he knew he wouldn't have the courage to kill himself if it got to a point where bills couldn't be paid. Someone would have to look after Woody, which was all that mattered, and he thought, then, of a life so unremarkable that he would disappear with no sign, remembered by a dog alone, assuming pets remembered their owners.

The breeze had begun to die down. Woody wanted to run, but there were still a few children around. There was also the possibility of some schoolteacher shouting about rules and animals. Mumbling about life in a police state, he held on to the leash firmly as Woody struggled to pull free. The dog crouched down suddenly, in the middle of the park, and Maynard realized he had forgotten to carry poop bags. He looked around, hoping no one would notice. There weren't too many adults; so, when Woody was done and moved away, he followed.

They had taken a few steps when he heard someone call out. He ignored it. 'Excuse me,' the person now shouted. 'Excuse me, sir.' It was a woman, which didn't surprise him. Why couldn't they mind their own business? He finally turned, after she kept calling, and found a short Asian lady, breathing heavily from the exertion of walking briskly up to him. 'Excuse me, sir,' she said again, as if he hadn't heard her the first five times. He looked down at her, and she waited for him to speak, but he said nothing.

'I've been calling you repeatedly, sir,' she said, while he continued to stare. Woody tugged at the leash, and he pulled, bringing the dog closer to him. 'You're supposed to clean up after your dog. You can't just walk away as if nothing happened. We all saw you. We were sitting right there. This is a public park and there are children who play here. You can't walk away from a mess your dog has created.' Her expression changed from confusion to anger as he stared at her in silence. 'I'm talking to you. Can you hear me? Hello?'

He smirked and turned away.

She didn't move, as if unsure of what to do, and then he heard her come after him. 'Excuse me. Excuse me. Do you think you can just pretend that none of this happened? I'm going to file a complaint. You people can't get away with this sort of thing.'

He turned around suddenly, and she stopped, her mouth still open. 'You people? What do you mean by *you people*?' he asked, his voice low and menacing. He wanted her to be afraid, but he also didn't want to lose his temper. It wouldn't do to scream, not while there were people around. It wouldn't do to punch her in the face, this bloody Asian woman. He was helpless, and they both knew it. *She* could yell at him if she wanted to, and he would be expected to shut up and take it. 'What do you mean by you people?' he asked again.

'You know exactly what I mean,' she said, regaining her composure and taking a step closer. She looked up into his face as if to tell him that she wasn't afraid. 'You dog owners treating public places like private property. You have to clean up after your pets. Did you not see the signs? There's one right at the entrance you walked through. Don't act as if you don't know the rules.'

'Are you saying I can't read? Are you saying I'm too stupid to understand the rules?'

'That's not what I said, sir. Don't put this on me. If you're trying to start an argument, that's fine, but it doesn't change what this is about. You brought your dog here and walked away without cleaning up. There are rules and you have to follow them.'

'Says who? Are you in charge of rules at this park? I didn't get the memo.'

'You think you can try and bully your way out of this, and I've seen it before. Please pick up after your dog. That is all I'm saying. Then we can both get on with our lives. I've got things to do.'

'If you really had things to do, you wouldn't be following dogs in parks, would you?'

'You're starting to get a little insulting, sir. I've said this before ... I will not hesitate to file a formal complaint.'

'With who? The Dog Cleaning Corporation of Forest Hills? There's no one in charge of cleaning up. Do it yourself if it bothers you.'

'With whom.'

'Excuse me?'

'Whom. You said "with who" but it's "whom". That's the correct thing to say.'

'This is an English lesson now? You're going to teach me how to speak my own language?'

'It's not an English lesson. You're being rude and clearly don't know how to speak.'

'I'll speak the way I want to, you fucking Asian bitch. Go back to China if you've got a problem with that.' He smiled as her mouth opened in shock, then turned, pulling Woody behind him.

'What the fuck did you just say to me?' he heard her say, then felt her hand tugging on his arm.

'Get your hands off me,' he said, raising his voice. Woody barked and came closer, sniffing the woman and looking up at Maynard. 'Back off before I set him on you.'

She opened her mouth in shock again, as if she wanted to say something but didn't know how.

He shrugged her hand off. 'Get out of my face and never speak to me again. Bitch.' He turned and began walking.

'You won't get away with this,' he heard her say. 'You can't speak to people like this. I'm calling the police.'

Still holding the leash, he lifted his right arm and held up his middle finger, his back still to her. Approaching the entrance to the park, he began to whistle, exhilarated. 'What a great day, huh, boy?' he said, looking down at Woody. He didn't look back to see if she was still there. He would have to take Woody to a park further down the road for a few days, but a walk never hurt anybody. Still whistling, he waited for the light to turn green, then crossed the road. Whoever she was, he hoped she wasn't following him.

JALANDHAR

11 APRIL 2018

It was unsettling how Rainak Bazar felt familiar yet strange at the same time. Sukhpreet knew the market hadn't changed, but he had. He walked a little more slowly than usual, as if to take in everything and store it away for a time when this would be a memory, stuck as if in amber. It made him feel like the director of a movie where he was the star, a thought that had come to him a few days ago in Chukhiara when he had gone to say goodbye. He wished he could have left from the village, but a taxi from Jalandhar was cheaper and he wasn't sure about walking into the airport without crying if his mother were to come along. To see her standing there without anyone would break him. This way, he could go alone, without someone seeing him off.

Harneet didn't say much as she walked beside him. She looked around too, as if trying to see the shops and people hurrying past through his eyes. They had met an hour earlier than usual, and she had skipped classes for the first time. He was happy to see her, and she sensed how much she would miss him.

'Are you sure about Toronto?'

'Sure? I have the visa and ticket. I leave in two days. How can I not be sure? What are you asking me? This was supposed to happen a year ago.'

'No, I mean, are you sure this is a good idea, to leave Jalandhar for a college you don't know anything about? What about those videos?'

'What videos?'

'The students who were going to be deported because their college was fake.'

'Deepanshu went to the same place.'

'But he didn't complete the course.'

'Who says I am going to complete the course? I'm just going there for one year before I drop out.'

'That's what I don't understand.'

'What don't you understand? I told you what the plan was. I can't believe we're having this conversation now, after my bags have been packed.'

'Why can't you get a real degree, so you can find a job?'

He laughed, then shook his head and kept walking. She looked at him as if to say something, then changed her mind. Reaching the end of the narrow lane, they turned, an automatic gesture, heading back towards the chaos of the market.

'I told you this before, but I don't know if you get it,' he said. 'We don't have the same lives or options. You can say things like "get a real degree" or "get a real job" because you have the opportunity to do both. I know you haven't received an acceptance letter yet, but it is just a matter of time. You know what I have: nothing. If I did, I would have been in Toronto last September. Instead, I saw my visa being rejected and I had to pay that agency for documents. What college with a good reputation will take someone like me? You know I scored 4.5 on the IELTS. You can apply to a proper college because you scored 6.5. And you can get a degree and a job, but how will I do that? I can't even speak English. Just hello, thank you, yes sir, no sir. Who will get a real job in Canada with that?'

She looked away, as if ashamed of what she had asked. 'I'm sorry. That is not what I meant.'

'Don't be sorry. I wish I could do what you asked, but you know how things are with people like us. If I don't go, what will I do here? What will I earn? How do I get my father's land from the bank?'

'I know. Let's talk about something else.'

'Okay, tell me about your plans.'

'What plans?'

'Education and career and life and any other plans.'

'I don't have any plans.'

'You're applying to universities in Canada and England, and you want to study further. These are good plans.'

'They are not my plans. You know that.'

'Okay, so this is what your parents want you to do.'

'Yes, it's what they have always wanted. They ask and I agree. Where is the question of me having plans of my own?'

'I'm asking what your plans would look like if your parents didn't insist on anything.'

'I tried thinking about this a few months ago, and the strange thing, or maybe the frightening thing, is that I couldn't come up with anything. My mind was a blank. It was as if I was incapable of thinking for myself. Isn't that sad?'

'No, it's not. Let's talk about that and see if we can both come up with a plan for you, instead of one created by your parents. You said you wanted to talk about something else.'

'Okay, let's talk about that.'

'Tell me what you liked when you were a child.'

'We have spoken about my childhood before ...'

'Yes, but we didn't speak about what you liked doing.'

'I liked the same things most children do. Eating, playing, dressing up ...'

'So, clothes, then.'

'Clothes? I don't know. I liked dressing up and looking nice. I don't think I do that anymore.'

'Are you saying you don't dress well or that you don't look nice anymore? Because both those things are untrue. You look nicer than anyone in Rainak Bazar.'

She looked up at him before turning away, and he thought he saw her blush.

'I don't know. Okay, I think I liked clothes.'

'Super. What about them? Do you still like them?'

'Yes, I can always tell when something is made well, or if someone should wear a different colour.'

'Tell me about my clothes. Does this shirt suit me?'

'No,' she laughed. 'Nothing you wear suits you.'

He laughed too. 'And you didn't say a word about it?'

'It never came up. You have never asked me something like this before.'

'So, what are you saying? That I look like a clown?'

She pushed him playfully and he moved closer. They looked at each other, and he wanted to imprint her face on his mind. It felt like something he would relive, that would sustain him. He wanted to tell her that but couldn't think of a way, so he continued to smile, as if for a passport photograph.

'Tell me what I should wear before I leave for Canada, so they don't laugh at me there.'

'You're very slim and you wear striped shirts, but they are the wrong kind of stripes.'

'Stripes are stripes. What are right stripes and wrong stripes?'

'Your stripes are vertical, so they make you look slimmer than you are. You should wear horizontal stripes because they will make you look a lot better.'

'More handsome?'

'No, just better.'

'So, I'm not handsome enough?'

'We were talking about my plans, not about whether you're handsome.'

'But since we're on the subject, and since I'm going soon, can you tell me, as a girl looking at a boy, if you think I'm handsome?'

'Why do you want to know?'

'Because I want to know what the gori women will think when they see me.'

'Do you want to marry a gori woman?'

'No, I want to marry a Punjaban, but I should know what the gori women think of me.'

'Why should it matter what they think of you if you're not interested in them?'

'Who said I was not interested? I said I wouldn't marry them.'

'I am not having this conversation.'

'Okay, let's go back to what you said. You like clothes and you can see what people should and shouldn't wear. What about studying that in college?'

'Studying what people wear?'

'No, getting a degree in fashion or design or textiles. I don't know.'

'A degree in fashion? What would I do with that?'

'You're smart. There's so much you can do with a degree like that. You could start a business, import-export, show people how to dress. There's so much you can do.'

'You're a dreamer.'

'I'm serious. Imagine being able to study what you like. What were you going to apply for?'

'I don't know. Papa was asking me to look at business development or human resources.'

'But you don't even know what those degrees mean.'

'He said they were the easiest to get into.'

'My diploma programme is on company practices, and I still don't know what it means.'

'But you don't care about studying. You just want a visa.'

'And you don't. So you can do something you really want to do.'

She didn't respond. There was music behind them, and they turned to see a small crowd walk down the street. Moving to the side, they watched as a procession of people chanting a hymn drifted past in single file—devotees heading towards a temple a kilometre-and-a-half away. Harneet stood close to Sukhpreet, their arms almost touching. He looked down at her, watching as she followed the procession, wishing he could place his arm around her. He didn't know when he would see her again, and the thought made him sadder than he thought it would. When the last devotee had moved past, they began walking again.

'Think about it.'

'About what?'

'Doing something you really want to instead of choosing a programme because your papa thinks it's a good idea.'

'If you meet my papa, you will know that he's a smart man.'

'I'm not saying anything about your papa or your parents. I know they want what is best for you. I'm asking you to think about what you want. There is nothing you can't do.'

'You sound like Shah Rukh Khan in that movie where he plays a hockey coach.'

'Okay, make fun of me and forget about your future.'

'Don't be mad. I'm listening to you. I will think about it. I promise.'

He looked at his watch. She would have to take the bus back in forty minutes or so. 'Do you want to stop for a lassi?'

'We just ate tikki less than half an hour ago.'

'Yes, but who knows when I will get Jalandhar lassi again.'

'That is a very good point. Let's go.'

They looked around for a restaurant that didn't seem too busy. There was Lassi Wala Dhaba, but Sukhpreet wanted a quieter place where they could speak, so they walked until they found Sunny Food Corner. There were a few people inside, but also an unoccupied table, and he nudged her towards it. It was at the far end, by a wall separating the eating area from the kitchen. Sitting down, he ordered two sweet lassis.

'When do you think we will meet again?'

'Next year, if you come to Toronto.'

'What if I don't get a visa?'

'How will you not get a visa? I managed one and I don't even have any real paperwork. Go and speak to that agent I went to. Deepanshu used him as well.'

'Agents say all kinds of things, but you know it's a lottery. You know what the consulate is like. What if the officer I speak to rejects me?'

'I thought the officer I spoke to was going to reject me a second time too, but I got lucky. He looked tired and I don't think he wanted to ask many questions. If you get someone who asks questions, you won't have to worry because you have the papers. Why are you afraid?'

'I have never lived anywhere on my own. I have never lived away from my parents. And now, in a year or two, I will be expected to be in another country, with people I don't know, working towards a degree in a language that is not my own. And you ask why I'm afraid?'

'Do you think this doesn't frighten me? I'm from a village. I can't even fit in here, in Jalandhar. I don't know what an airplane looks like on the inside. But I can't just sit here and grow old and watch my mother lose the little she has. So, I'm going and doing whatever it takes to survive. I won't eat if there is no food. I will clean toilets if I have to. I'll sleep on the floor of Deepanshu's room if I can't afford a place. I don't know what Canada is going to be like, but it will be better than here. I sent you those videos. You saw the cars they drive there, and the lives they have. Don't you want that?'

'I've seen the videos, Sukhpreet, but I don't know if I believe them. I have also heard other things about students in Canada. Maybe you don't want to think about it, but I have heard frightening stuff. My parents know of students who haven't returned, and some who come back in boxes. Videos show a lot of things, but I have to see them with my own eyes.'

'Deepanshu wouldn't lie to me. He's like my brother. He wants me to come there because he says it's better and I want to believe him.'

'Is Punjab really so bad? Be honest and tell me what is wrong with this place. Yes, it's crowded and noisy and dirty, but it's also full of life and there is happiness. Why go to a country where no one knows you just because the streets look cleaner and the buildings are taller?'

'You ask me this again and again, and I keep telling you we have to try making our lives better. To stay here is to do what our parents did. If we go, even if things don't work for us, maybe they will work for our children and those who come after us.'

'I don't think we will ever agree on that, but what can I say? I'm applying too, so maybe I don't have any right to ask about your decision.'

'You can ask me anything. You have a right to say anything without worrying about what I think.'

'Why do I have that right?'

'I think you know.'

'Know what?'

'You're just teasing me.'

'No, I'm serious. What right do I have and why?'

'Harneet, I ...'

'If you want to say something, say it. You're going in a few days.'

'You know how I feel about you.'

'That's what you want to say?'

'You know what I want to say but I can't say it.'

'Why? Are you shy?'

'You know I am. But I want you to know that I am asking you to come to Canada for a reason.'

'For a better life?'

'Yes, but no.'

'Not a better life?'

'I want you to come and have a better life with me.'

She smiled, shielding her face behind the glass of lassi. He smiled too, and they both laughed. She reached out and touched his wrist.

'I'm coming to Toronto, and I will see you in Brampton, in that big house you will have.'

'I will come and pick you up from the airport in my car.'

'And how will you have that car in a year? By stealing from a bank?'

'No, from the job I will get in six months. Wait and watch.'

She shook her head and looked away, and he stared at the half-full glass before him. It felt odd, this awkwardness with the only person he had ever felt comfortable with. A waiter came by, asking if they wanted anything else, and they shook their heads. Sukhpreet signalled for the bill. It arrived in a small plastic bowl, stuck into a pile of fennel seeds. He reached for his wallet and removed a few notes, putting them into the bowl.

'I wish I could come to the airport with you.'

'The flight is at 1.20 a.m. and I'm going alone. Your parents will kill you if you go out at midnight.'

'I wish I could have taken you to meet them.'

'They would never let you bring some boy home.'

'I know, that's why I said I *wished* I could.'

'That's also why we have to leave.'

'Because of my parents?'

'No, because we deserve to be able to make our own choices. We don't have to go where we are told or marry whom we are asked to.'

'Are you thinking about marrying someone?'

He laughed again, shaking his head. 'I'm too young to think about marriage. but when I have a job and I am ready, I know whom to ask.'

'Someone from Chukhiara?'

'Someone from Jalandhar.'

She slapped him on the wrist, and he leaned back. He looked around at the restaurant, at the dirty plates abandoned on a table beside them, as the cashier adjusted a framed photograph of Guru Nanak Dev Ji. He breathed in deeply.

'What happens now?'

'What do you mean? After we drink our lassi?'

'No, after you reach Toronto.'

'Deepanshu will meet me at the airport and take me to his room.'

'Have you seen the room? On WhatsApp?'

'I asked him to show it to me, but he always calls when he's outside. I'm sure it's a nice place.'

'You should have asked him to show it to you. You should know where you're going to live, and what the room looks like.'

'How does it matter? Nothing can be worse than living at the hostel, so why worry about Deepanshu's place?'

Pushing her glass away, she looked up at him and smiled, a little sadly. 'When will we meet again?'

'Soon. In a year or two. When you're in Toronto.'

'What if that doesn't happen?'

'Why won't it happen? You finish college in a few months and you're going to keep applying.'

'Yes, but what if it doesn't happen?'

'Why think about those things when there is no reason to?'

'Because we can't predict where life will take us or how things may change.'

'It will happen. I'm going there, studying for a few months, dropping out of college and starting work. And then I will find a place of my own.'

'You don't even know if that is possible or legal.'

'Deepanshu did it. He's going to get his PR card soon. Permanent Resident of Canada. That is what I'm going to get.'

'But you have never been outside India. Or even outside Jalandhar. How are you so sure?'

'Why are you always critical?' he asked, slapping the table forcefully. Harneet sat back with a start, and he apologized immediately.

'Sorry, sorry. I'm not angry. I'm just ... why are you always asking me questions when you know I have no answers? Yes, I have never been outside Jalandhar. What do you get by reminding me of it? Do you think I am sure about Toronto or Canada or Brampton or the college I'm going to, or whether Deepanshu has a bed for me, or whether I can leave college and work without a permit? I don't know anything. I just know I have a visa, a ticket and an acceptance letter, and I am going to try. That is all we can do. Trust in god and try. What is wrong with that?'

She reached out and touched his hand again. 'I'm sorry. I am just worried.'

He gently removed his hand from under hers. Rubbing his face, he closed his eyes for a few seconds before opening them. She looked upset, and he placed his hand on hers again.

'I'm afraid. I even don't know what to do at the airport. I don't know where I have to go, or who will look at my passport and how I will find my plane. I don't know how I will get off the plane in one country and take a second plane, and what visa officers will ask me in Canada. I don't know where my bags will go and how I will get them back. I don't think about it because Deepanshu did it, so many people from Chukhiara have done it ... so I can, too. Which is how I know you will do it.'

She nodded, saying nothing, and they sat for a while with empty glasses until the waiter returned and picked them up, along with the crisp notes.

'I sometimes ask myself if this will be the biggest mistake of my life.'

'What? Applying for a visa or coming to meet me in Canada?'

'Just this new life I am going to choose by leaving everything behind.'

'How will you know until you leave? What if you stay and think about why you didn't leave?'

'It's not as if I am not going to leave, but I still think to myself—I'm happy here. I like my college and life with my parents. I see the girls who leave and how they change when they come back.'

'How do they change? They wear expensive clothes and speak Punjabi with an accent?'

'Yes, but not just that. I feel as if they carry something inside them, a kind of emptiness. They frighten me.'

'I don't understand what you're saying.'

'My cousin Manpreet went to Birmingham three years ago. She got married and has two children.'

'Okay, and?'

'She came back to Jalandhar because her mother, my maasi, had a bypass. She stayed for two weeks and came to see us before she returned to England. I have known Manpreet since we were little, and this person sitting in our living room was someone else. My parents were pleased to see her, and she showed us pictures of her house and told us to come and visit her.'

'So, what frightened you? What did she say?'

'Nothing she said seemed real. She laughed a lot and spoke about London and how they were planning to go to France for her son's birthday. When my parents went to the kitchen, I asked if she was happy, and she just laughed again.'

'And the way she laughed made you feel as if she was lying?'

'No, it made me feel as if there was something she wasn't telling me. Something about her life or her children. I don't know. It was just a feeling. When she got up to leave, she hugged us all, and held me tight for a few seconds, and I could just sense that something was wrong.'

'Do you call or speak to her?'

'She doesn't chat much. She sends photographs of her children when I message her on WhatsApp, but we have never called or done a video chat. When she is in Birmingham, it's as if she disappears into some other life. I don't know'

'Do you worry that you will turn into some other kind of person if you go to Canada?'

'I worry that I will forget who I really am.'

'You sound like a philosopher. Going to a foreign country always changes everyone.'

'Yes … I can't explain. When I met my cousin, I didn't see a person who was comfortable … in the way I am comfortable being Harneet or you are comfortable being Sukhpreet.'

'Now you sound like this professor at my college who is always …'

'Forget it, it's too confusing.'

He began to say something, then shook his head.

'I told you I was afraid,' he said, 'and I think I understand what you're saying, but I promise I won't change. Canada will not make me someone else.'

'I'm not worried about that,' she replied, smiling.

'This lassi was super.'

'I love how you say super.'

'What is wrong with super?'

'It is just funny. I hear you say it often, but always forget to mention it. I remember you saying it when we first met. Super.'

'It means great or good.'

'I know what it means, Sukhpreet. I just don't know anyone else who uses it. One English word for everything that is good.'

'You're making fun of my English now. Just because you scored more in your IELTS.'

'God, I don't want to think about the IELTS. Okay, fine, super. Super.'

'See? You will like the word too.'

'I like it already. I'm going to start using it when you're gone.'

He smiled. They sat in silence until the waiter walked up again to ask if they wanted anything. Standing up, they edged their way out from behind the tables. Once outside, Sukhpreet checked his watch. Harneet would have to leave in ten minutes, and it struck him, as if for the first time, that neither of them knew when they would meet again like this, in this market, for aloo tikki and a lassi. When he turned, she was looking down at her feet.

They waited for the bus, still silent. When it arrived, she looked at him and reached for his face with her palm, stroking his cheek gently before dropping her hand. He watched the bus pull away and move down the street, wondering if he should have said something or made a gesture that would stay with her, but nothing came to mind, and he hated that these ideas all came from Bollywood movies. She would have found it cheesy too, so he continued to watch until the bus turned a corner. Walking in the other direction, he crossed the street and headed for his own bus that would take him to the hostel.

It was quiet when he arrived, the door locked. Stepping into the room, he switched on the tube light. His two suitcases stood where he had left them earlier that day, by the side of his bed. His roommates had wanted to throw him a party, which surprised him, but he demurred if only to make sure his last few days would be uneventful. There had been a surge of respect in the way they addressed him after finding out that he was leaving. One of them had begun getting him food, while the other had asked for his IELTS notes.

He knew his roommates had applied too, but didn't know if they were trying to get to Canada or Australia. He also knew they had failed to score enough on their IELTS and had to take it a third time. He overheard one of them mention an agent who could take the test on his behalf for 1,50,000 rupees; the amount shocked him. The only explanation was land, and how much of it their parents were willing to mortgage. He thought of how much land had been sold by so many, for so long, and how Punjab would one day be a state where the fields would no longer be green. There would be no one left to till them, and he saw himself returning to a village he would no longer recognize. He had heard of people losing their land after being unable to pay back mortgages and knew Deepanshu still had years to go before his parents could recover what they had put up as collateral. He wanted his mother to get back everything, because that was the land his father had worked on. It had been cultivated by his blood, and by the blood of his ancestors.

Sitting down on the bed, he pushed aside a few dirty clothes that needed to be washed before he could pack them away. His phone pinged, and he pulled it from his pocket. It was a message from Harneet. 'I am home,' it said. 'Come home soon.'

A tear trickled out, surprising him as it rolled down his nose and fell onto the front of his shirt. His thumb hovered over the phone as he thought of what he could say. '*Rabb rakha*,' he typed. May god protect you. There were two blue ticks as she read his message. He waited to see if she would reply, but there was nothing. Putting away the phone, he leaned back on the bed, closing his eyes.

TORONTO

18 FEBRUARY 2019

Maynard ignored the knock at the door. He was in the bedroom, his eyes closed, and back against the wall. Woody barked, then went to the living room. There were more knocks, followed by silence. He opened his eyes after a few minutes. Outside, he noticed the envelope that had been pushed through the letterbox. He let it lie there and went to the kitchen, where he filled a glass of water. After a few slow sips, he poured the rest out and put down the glass, before walking out to pick up the envelope. It had the Beltway Properties letterhead, and he placed it unopened on the table, on top of a small pile of other envelopes.

They were all notices threatening eviction, and he knew Diego would return every morning until he spoke to him. Rubbing his eyes, he yawned, trying to remember the last time he had slept for eight straight hours. He had stayed up until 3 a.m., looking up information on how he could protect himself as a tenant. The company couldn't just throw him out. There was always a backlog at the Landlord and Tenant Board, and he read about tenants who had managed to stay on for six months after being served eviction notices. All comments online closed with the same warning though: it was just a matter of time.

He thought of starting an online petition, but couldn't think of what to write on it. Why would anyone give a forty-nine-year-old white man money for no reason? There was no life-threatening disease he could claim, and no act of injustice he could complain about, even though he couldn't think of anything in his life that seemed fair. Matters wouldn't have come to this if it weren't for Woody's operation, but who would care enough about that to send him money? There were always dog-lovers who would empathize, but would they support a stranger? He certainly wouldn't if the tables were turned. He would assume it was just another scam.

Woody came up to where he stood and sat at his usual spot under the table. The fur on his back had begun to grow back, but the ugly scar running diagonally across was still plainly visible. Maynard sat down and stroked the dog's head. It wasn't his fault. The veterinarian had suggested putting him down, and Maynard had almost assaulted him, knowing he wouldn't have dared mention it if he had insurance. He was still angry about it, the thought of letting Woody go just because he didn't have the means to make sure he would be okay. How were people supposed to have children when Canadians couldn't even take care of pets?

He wanted to speak to someone at Beltway and come up with a payment plan that allowed him to send in half the rent with interest, but they would never agree. To them, he was a liability protected by the Rent Control Act, someone they couldn't wait to see the last of. When he was gone, they would repaint his condo and put it on the market for $1000 more, and it would be snapped up within days given how hard it was for people to find accommodation near good schools.

He would have reached out to his sister, but wasn't sure if her Hotmail address was still operational. He couldn't remember the last time they had messaged each other. The only way out was a job, but nothing he had looked at over the past few weeks seemed promising. He wouldn't be able to explain why he hadn't worked for years. It felt as if he had fallen down a crack, and the world had simply decided to step over him and move on. Switching on his computer, he stared at the screen as it flickered and came slowly to life. He would have to look for blue collar jobs, and it frightened him. What would he do in the event of an injury? What if his back gave way? How would he take care of himself as well as Woody? His lower lip quivered, and he thought he would cry. Woody looked up and whined softly, as if sensing that something was wrong. Maynard reached down and rubbed his head. 'Nothing's going to happen,' he said softly. 'We'll figure this out. We always do, remember?'

The dog closed his eyes again. He would have to take him for a walk soon, but wanted to wait until Diego wasn't in the office. If he was lucky, the super would be on his rounds, attending to maintenance tasks. He had managed to slip out over the past week, but his luck wouldn't last forever. He would have to find a way of dealing with this humiliation. He could picture the smile on the man's face. He imagined him going back to his own condo and telling his wife about the poor white loser who couldn't pay rent. They would laugh and say something about lazy Canadians, and he clenched his fist. He had to get through that conversation without losing his temper.

It was anger—his inability to control his emotions—that had brought him to this. It would finish him too, some day, when everything boiled over and made him choose violence over temperance. He wished he had a way of smothering his combative urges, but it was useless. They lay below the surface, threatening to rise at the smallest provocation. It was like a low-grade fever, and he could feel his face flush as if his temperature was always rising. It happened more often these days, and it frightened him, this inability to take a walk without wanting to harm something or someone.

Turning to the computer, he double-clicked the browser and searched for job sites. Local grocery stores were short-staffed but would prefer someone younger. More of them now hired international students, and he thought of his own time as a high schooler, when working at a Timmie's or Trader Joe's in summer was a great way of putting aside money to enjoy the rest of the year. All that changed when the government changed the rules around work permits. He couldn't recall if it was Harper's time, or Trudeau's, but that hardly mattered. They were all the same, the whole sorry lot of them.

He was tempted to post something on Reddit, then decided to keep looking for jobs instead. All he needed was one manager willing to take him on, someone who didn't care about ridiculous things like diversity. All he needed was a Canadian willing to help another Canadian. He typed in 'customer service' and scrolled through the vacancies. The last one, posted four days ago, was a six-month contract for an 'Outdoor Sales Representative' offering $20 an hour. He read the list of requirements, mentally ticking off what he could and couldn't do. The role asked for 'previous experience in sales, marketing and customer service,' which he wasn't sure he possessed. It also required a criminal record check, punctuality, and the need for candidates to conduct themselves with integrity. 'You must enjoy working with and talking to people' it continued, and must be 'energetic and self-motivated, with a strong desire to achieve your goals.' Nothing about the post explained what the actual job was. What were these sales representatives supposed to sell? What was the product? Why did they want criminal checks for something that paid $20 an hour? It was frustrating. He attached his resume anyway and clicked the 'submit' button.

It was the same thing, day after day, and he realized he must have applied to over a hundred positions over the past few weeks. Half were roles he had no prior experience in, but there was little he could do besides walking to stores in his neighbourhood and asking if they were hiring.

Woody whined again, and he turned away from the computer. 'Okay, fine, let's go,' he said, standing up and heading to the bedroom for the leash. He placed it gently on the dog, making sure it didn't touch the scar. There was a check-up with the veterinarian scheduled for that weekend. He could apply for a new credit card, but banks knew everyone's credit score these days. They would not give him one until he repaid the amount owed on three older cards.

Pulling on his shoes, he reached for a jacket and opened the door. The passageway was empty. He walked down slowly, making sure the leash wasn't pulling Woody, and reached the ground floor. Stepping into the lobby, he was relieved to find Diego's office door shut. He was tempted to run out, then stopped. It was ridiculous to be so afraid. Diego was just a super, not someone deserving of respect. Outside, it was chilly, but pleasant, and he breathed in deeply. The thought of another winter storm made him panic. He imagined himself at the side of some road a few years from now, his belongings in cardboard boxes around him, holding Woody for warmth.

How was it possible, he asked himself again, a question that kept him up every night. How was he so close to homelessness after years of staying afloat? Reaching the end of the street, he stopped for the red light, looking down at Woody. He felt a sudden surge of affection and closed his eyes, trying to picture a future for himself and this dog who trusted him. Would they begin the next year in a homeless shelter? Even leaving Toronto was no longer an option, given how much a moving company would charge to pack and transport his meagre possessions to a less expensive city. And where were the less expensive cities in Canada? Grocery bills were the same everywhere. The only thing that changed, if at all, was the cost of a condo. For Canadians like him, people who would never own property, one city was as good or bad as the other.

The light changed and he entered the park, waiting for Woody to go behind a bush. He hadn't bothered to carry a bag and didn't care if anyone saw him. It was alarming how he no longer feared anyone except the superintendent of his building. It made him feel as if on the edge of something new, an invisible threshold that would liberate him or tip him into an unknown space.

When Woody was done, he continued walking, the dog panting slightly behind him. The children were at school and there were few adults. He thought of removing the leash but didn't. It could be a few weeks before Woody felt strong enough to run, and that relief was tempered by what he knew the veterinarian would charge. Maybe he shouldn't have brought a dog into his life, but not waking up to see Woody beside him was too much to bear, and he regretted the thought immediately.

The park had a running track around it, now empty. Stopping now and again for Woody to catch up, he thought of what he looked like to passersby: skinny white man with a beer belly, not very tall, a face that was instantly forgettable. It was like the male version of a cat lady, thc kind his friends had made fun of while growing up. Where were they now? Did they make it out okay, with families and cars, a townhouse in the city and cottage in the country? That was the dream for so many of them, even though it didn't seem like it at the time. It was a perfectly ordinary life, easily accessible to anyone who put their heads down and worked hard. When had it given way to this nightmare where healthcare and a roof could no longer be taken for granted?

His phone rang, startling him. No one had his number, and he assumed it was from the building's office, calling to ask about rent. He was tempted to ignore the call, but at last, accepted it, ready to be as belligerent as possible if it meant buying some time.

'Is this Mr Wilson?'

'Who is it?'

'I'm calling from the Reed Staffing Company in Ottawa. This is about your application for the role of forklift operator. Is this a good time to chat?'

He didn't respond, trying to remember when he had applied. He had never driven a forklift.

'Yes, it's a great time. Do you want me to come in for an interview or something?'

'No, I just want to clarify a few details first. I have a couple of questions if that's okay?'

'Sure.'

'Could you tell me about your previous experience with warehousing? I looked at your resume, but everything was related to customer service or front office duties, and there was nothing about working at a factory. You do know this requires the managing of forklift duties for large goods. Could you tell me a little about your experience on that front?'

'I don't have much experience, but I'm happy to learn. What does it pay?'

'That's not how this works, Mr Wilson. This is a screening call to shortlist candidates, and I'm afraid I can't send your resume forward because you aren't qualified for the role.'

'It's just a forklift. How hard can it be? I drove a car for twenty years,' he said roughly, before calming down. 'Look, I get it, but I'll take any other role you have, anything that involves supervising people on a factory floor or a store. I've worked with Canadian Tire and Home Depot, and a bunch of those guys. This isn't that much of a stretch for me.'

'I understand, Mr Wilson, and I will be happy to send your resume across to some of my colleagues who are looking to fill those roles. I'm afraid you won't be a good fit for this one though. Thanks for your time. Have a nice day.'

'What about ...'

He was cut off abruptly, and held the phone away from his ear, looking at it as if the caller had slammed a door in his face. For a second, he was tempted to throw it to the ground.

Then, putting it back into his pocket, he began walking again, breathing heavily as he felt a surge of anger.

By the time he completed a full circle of the park, Woody was tired. He didn't have much energy because the antibiotics were strong enough to knock him out. Bending down, Maynard picked up the dog and carried him, moving towards the park entrance. He was glad of the short walk because Woody was heavier. It had been years since he last carried him, and that made him sad. Sometimes, he could see the two of them hurtling down an empty tunnel with no guiding light.

Standing at the signal, he saw a few people step out from his building. He had seen them before, but they offered no sign of recognition. They had long given up greeting him. He hadn't spoken to anyone here for years, which was a mistake. Maybe a friendly neighbour could have helped at a time like this.

Crossing the street, he walked to the building and gently placed Woody on the ground. It had been less than a half hour since they had left, and he reminded himself to tell the veterinarian about Woody's exhaustion. As they entered, he noticed that Diego's office was open. He could hear the superintendent speaking to another resident and hurried past hoping he wouldn't be spotted. If Diego noticed, he didn't shout out. Pushing open the door to the stairwell, Maynard walked up the stairs with Woody in his arms again. He entered the condo, placed Woody down and leaned back against the closed door. He couldn't avoid Diego forever.

He removed the leash, walked to the bedroom to put it away, then carried Woody into the bathroom, placing him in the bathtub so he could wash his paws. As he dried them, there was a knock.

He opened the door to Diego.

'What is it?'

'The rent, sir.'

It was the way he said 'sir' that made Maynard feel the contempt with which the superintendent regarded him. There was no respect in the greeting, and the word was spat out.

'What about the rent? I'll pay it. You should tell your boss or your bosses that sending me multiple letters doesn't change anything. I'll pay. It's coming.'

Diego didn't respond. He folded his arms and stared at Maynard, who felt an urge to slam the door. Woody came up and stood between his legs, his tongue wagging.

'If you don't pay within one week, we will have to start the eviction process.'

Maynard stared at him, then shut the door. There was another knock. He waited until Diego knocked again, then opened it.

'I heard you.'

'Sir, after one week, I will bring a formal letter of eviction.'

'I got your message the first time. You don't need to come back. You'll get your rent by next week.'

Diego didn't reply and walked away, as Maynard banged the door close. He paced the living room. This wasn't the situation he had in mind. He wanted a civil conversation with someone from the company who could come up with a repayment plan. He had let his anger get the better of him, but suspected Diego would do nothing to encourage any negotiation. He knew the superintendent probably had no right to consider offers from tenants, but Maynard had let the opportunity go. He was left with no option but to find the rent in seven days. He wanted the money more than ever, if only to throw down the cheque in front of that smug little Mexican's face.

Walking to his desk, he switched on his computer. Woody whined, and Maynard looked down at him, waving his finger. The dog was hungry but could wait. He Googled 'pawn shops near me' and scrolled through the list. All he had were a few pieces of jewellery that belonged to his mother, things he had held on to because he was afraid of finding out how authentic they were. He had split them with his sister, each of them taking two necklaces along with some brooches. He wished he could find out if she had sold them and what they were worth. The colour of the jewellery hadn't changed in years, which he hoped was a good sign. If they were worth something, maybe they could cover not just the rent for the months he had missed, but tide him through a few more weeks, until he could find a job.

He dialled a number for the first shop, explaining what he wanted to pawn and making an appointment for the following morning. Then he called two more shops. They all said he could walk in, but he insisted on appointments. Maybe it would convince them that he had something genuinely valuable and coerce them into making a better offer. Putting down his phone, he stood up, walking to the kitchen and returning with Woody's steel bowl. As the dog chewed his food, Maynard scrolled through job listings. He would have to take anything that was offered. Closing his eyes, he thought about how long he could survive on minimum wage.

Clicking open a new tab, he logged onto Pornhub. It upset him that he couldn't even masturbate as often as he used to; he knew his low libido had everything to do with depression. He looked at the categories he used to prefer: 'Japanese Massage', 'Latino Casting', 'Stepmom and Son', and clicked on the first one. It opened a new page, multiple videos in neat rows, each thumbnail depicting a nude or half-clothed Asian woman on a table. He watched as a male masseur fondled a woman's breasts. The sound was turned off, and he imagined her moaning, then rubbed his groin. He felt nothing, but continued to rub it, hoping for some sign of pleasure, if only for a few seconds. He pictured himself looking in from the outside, a misshapen man before a computer, a dog at his foot, watching pornography in a featureless room.

Stopping the video, he picked up his phone again, scrolling through his contacts. Diego picked up and Maynard identified himself. If the superintendent was surprised, he said nothing.

'I'm sorry I was rude. I'm hoping we can try and resolve this without it becoming ugly.'

'Ugly?'

'An ugly situation. I mean, I don't want this to create any issues between us or the management.'

'You have to pay rent. If you don't, the building will evict you. Nothing I can do.'

'I understand, but I was hoping we could find an arrangement without bothering the head office.'

'What arrangement? I cannot let you stay without rent.'

'I'm not asking you to. I will have the rent money in a few days, but I am thinking of another arrangement that can help us both.'

'What kind of arrangement?'

'I know you need help.'

'Help with what?'

'With the building. You had a notice on the office board a few days ago, an ad for an assistant. You don't have an assistant yet. Are you still looking for one?'

'You want to be my assistant? Assistant superintendent?'

'I'm looking for a way of making sure I can continue to stay. You know I have been here for many years now. How long have you been staying here?'

'Almost four years.'

'I have been around for much longer. I know the building. I know the job and what needs to be done. I could help in all kinds of ways.'

'You want me to hire you?'

'That's exactly right. Hire me as your assistant, and the building can deduct a portion of my salary towards rent. We both get help until I can figure out what to do. You don't have anyone yet.'

The silence meant Diego was thinking about the offer. Maynard was surprised at himself. He had no intention of applying for anything when he called, until that advertisement had popped into his head while imagining Diego in the office below. The more he thought about it, the smarter it sounded. It would kill him to call Diego his boss, but it would mean being able to live without worrying about rent. If this went well and he did a great job, maybe he could take Diego's place within a few years. Suddenly excited, he began pacing the length of the room.

'You can come and talk to me about this,' the superintendent said at last. 'You need to understand the job and make a formal application.'

'Of course. I will come with my resume. I have solid experience at Canadian Tire and also ...'

'You have no experience as superintendent.'

'Yes, I understand, but that's why I was telling you about the years I have lived here. I knew the superintendent before you, and the one before him. I know what they did. I understand the job better than anyone else because I know this building. I know which dryer doesn't work well, and which condo has a problem with roaches. I'm perfect for the job.'

'You have never said this before. You have never spoken about this. You only complain.'

'Yes, I apologize. I know that. I'm trying to fix this situation not just for me but for you as well. Your life will be easier with an assistant, and I will get a chance to figure out this rent issue. You know things have been difficult for me for a while now.'

Diego was silent again.

'Come down and we can talk about this.'

'Do you want me to come today or make an appointment for tomorrow morning?'

'Tomorrow is not good. Day after at 10 a.m. is good.'

'Great. See you the day after. Thanks, Diego. You have a great day.'

The superintendent hung up without responding to his greeting, but Maynard didn't care. He put the phone down and walked to his window that overlooked the parking lot. Staring at a small patch of sky to the right, between two other buildings, he felt better than he had in days. Part of him still bristled at what he would have to do to convince Diego. It would mean swallowing his pride, but he would do it for Woody. He had no expectations of insurance from the job but, at the very least, it would give them both time. He knew it would be hard for the company to find an assistant on the pittance they were probably offering. He considered emailing the head office, then decided not to. Diego's recommendation would be more convincing if he got through that interview. All he had to do, until then, was go to the pawn shop and hope that his mother's jewellery would be enough to save them for a few more weeks.

Turning around, he walked to where Woody lay and stroked his head. The dog looked up, then licked his arm. For the first time in weeks, Maynard laughed.

TORONTO

14 JULY 2019

It took Sukhpreet a few seconds to identify the low rumble in the room as the sound of Deepanshu snoring. He was disoriented, the drawn blinds making it difficult to figure out the time. Sitting up slowly, he yawned, irritated at being woken up even though he knew it wasn't Deepanshu's fault. His cousin had begun working the night shift at a gas station, often returning just after Sukhpreet had finally managed to fall asleep. Their arrangement with the condo owner allowed him to share the room, but one of them had to sleep on the floor. There was no space for a larger bed, and Sukhpreet now knew that renting a place of their own would take them years, given what they were being paid.

He walked to the window and pushed aside the blinds. Retrieving his phone from a small table by the bed, he saw that it was 7 a.m. and already bright outside. It was startling to imagine how this would change in a few months, when another winter in Canada would arrive like an unwelcome visitor. He remembered how excited he had been at the prospect of seeing snow, but that was in Jalandhar, in what felt like another world, even though it wasn't that long ago. Leaning against the wall, he let the drapes close and turned to look at Deepanshu curled under a blanket.

He sometimes felt like leaving his cousin, even though he had nowhere to go, and knew the feeling stemmed from frustration and resentment. It wasn't Deepanshu's fault that Brampton was not what he had made it out to be. It was his own fault, his own need for validation that had prompted him to create this fantasy. To chastise Deepanshu was easy because he was the only tangible link between what he had left behind and the uncertainty of what he had stepped into. He had known Canada would be difficult and, if he struggled, he alone was to blame.

Deepanshu worked constantly, and Sukhpreet saw how much his cousin had been counting on his presence here. Maybe he had a fantasy of his own, of two salaries being enough for a condominium. Neither had accounted for a constant stream of students from Punjab who chose Brampton, competing not just for rooms, but for beds in basements.

He remembered reading somewhere that over 1,00,000 international students had entered Canada that year alone. It was supposed to be an all-time high but meant little as a statistic. He could see how it affected his daily life, on days when he walked the streets after his classes were finished, handing out his resume to stores, restaurants, and any business that looked as if it would hire someone part-time. He should have seen it that first day in college, how everyone in his class as well as every other class in the building, was brown. 'Where are the goras?' he had asked Deepanshu, who laughed.

Surprise had slowly given way to shock, followed by a dull anger that settled and refused to budge, no matter how much he tried to be optimistic. The college had no full-time teachers for most courses offered, and he could see how little his efforts mattered. He had no intention of continuing beyond the first year but wondered about classmates who clearly looked at the diploma as a stepping stone to something bigger. He wanted to ask why they didn't say anything to the college management, and why they were okay with losing huge amounts of money. After a few months, he realized what they must have understood long before he did. To provoke a shift in this country required still more money, which no one could afford. It was strange how even asking for basic rights meant having to pay someone a fee to represent those interests. To complain meant risking the visa, and that stamp meant more than anything else. So, everyone chose silence.

There were conversations with Deepanshu that would end with his cousin shaking his head and leaving, with Sukhpreet wondering if he was the only person who didn't understand what was going on in this country. Did everyone know it was a lie except him? Where were the easy part-time jobs for weekends at the mall? He skipped lunch on most weekdays for the first seven months at college, until he found Kwality Kitchen, a restaurant that allowed him to work for more than the twenty hours he was legally allowed. The downside was he had no way of asking its owners to pay him what they were supposed to. And so, for less than $10 an hour, he would skip half his classes and do everything from washing dishes, to refilling bottles of ketchup and wiping down tables. Twenty hours moved to thirty, then forty, as he began cutting down on more classes. He was sure the college knew, but most of his classmates had been missing for months by the time he stopped going. Their fees had been paid, and none of the teachers complained.

A sound distracted Sukhpreet. Deepanshu had stirred, mumbling in his sleep. He did it often, but always claimed not to remember what he had dreamed about. He knew his cousin was unhappy, and Sukhpreet grew sad when he considered how well Deepanshu had managed to conceal that unhappiness from everyone for so long. When they were young, Deepanshu would walk into a room and get others to dance. He was like a jolt of energy, forcing life into those who stumbled into his orbit. Now, when Sukhpreet saw him, he was reminded of the taxi drivers who stood outside Jalandhar railway station, waiting for passengers in silence. Deepanshu was barely twenty-six but looked like a man twice his age.

Checking his phone again, he saw that it was 7.15 a.m. He began rolling up his blanket and mattress. He had found a job at a convenience store in Toronto, which required him to leave by 8.30 a.m. for a nine-hour shift that began at 10.30. He had classmates who attended classes, then rode buses to work at factories for six hours, before getting home after midnight, for six days a week. He admired them, but wondered how long it would take for them to break. He had come close to it on numerous occasions, feeling tears well up without warning while doing mundane things. He didn't even know what he was weeping for, only that there was an ache that nothing could heal, a longing for something that he knew was no longer in his possession.

Leaving the room, he walked outside as softly as possible and pulled the door shut. There were two other roommates, both working late hours. Sukhpreet showered, then sat in the empty kitchen with two slices of buttered bread and a cup of tea. The GO train from Brampton Bus Terminal to Bloor took a little over an hour, but it also took him a half hour to get to the terminal. Missing the train meant losing hours at work, and Sukhpreet had only missed it once over his four months at the store. After gulping down his tea, he rinsed the cup and plate, packed a parantha from the night before for lunch, picked up his rucksack and walked out.

He zipped up his jacket for the ten-minute walk to the bus stop. Deepanshu had mentioned buying new boots before the snow arrived, and he wanted to see what they cost at the city malls, so he would know what prices to expect. As the bus rolled into view, he joined a small crowd and pushed his way through. There were more students now than when he had first arrived, and he had heard of buses driving past because they couldn't pack in more people. It was the same at the GO station. Where it was once possible to buy a ticket a few minutes before a train, there were now lines outside counters and vending machines.

The bus moved slowly, with fourteen stops before the Brampton terminal. All he could hear was Punjabi or Hindi, and the languages comforted him, weaving a net that would start to fray as he approached Toronto. The city still made him anxious, which he hadn't mentioned to Deepanshu who would have been amused. He couldn't explain what he was afraid of, except that it was palpable, the unease as his train approached Bloor, and a dryness in his throat until the ride home. He was sure his cousin felt it too, even if he would never admit to it. There were still a few minutes for the train, and he walked the length of the platform looking for a less crowded spot.

These days, everywhere he looked, there were more and more bicycles; this puzzled him, until Deepanshu explained. Students from Brampton who worked for online delivery apps preferred travelling to the city because the chances of tips were higher. His cousin no longer worked for the company he had spent five years with, saying it wasn't worth the effort. Sukhpreet could only imagine how limited the options were for students, forced to spend time and money with companies that wouldn't even guarantee a minimum wage. He said a short prayer, thanking Waheguru for his job. There were no benefits, and he still earned less than someone with a work visa or permanent residency card, but it was a job. The convenience store was owned by a middle-aged Chinese man who only hired students because of how little he had to pay them. He hadn't even asked Sukhpreet about experience and paid in cash every two weeks. Sukhpreet kept applying to other jobs, asking Harneet to check his applications for spelling errors before sending them out.

Stepping into the train, he found more bicycles, squeezing past them while trying to find a seat. The compartment was full, and almost entirely occupied by young men. He thought about what they had all been through to find themselves here on this train. There were the ghosts of families behind them, parents who had saved money or mortgaged homes to send their children to this new world. He was here, with them, because he believed in the same thing, but found that each day left him with more questions than answers.

The train rolled past smaller suburbs and sudden stretches of fields. He spotted two horses on one of them, the sight cheering him up. When he turned away, he realized that no one else was looking out. Most of them were napping or staring into phones. He caught snatches of conversation, about salaries and politics, which depressed him. Where his early days in Brampton would find him gravitating towards these discussions, they now made him feel as if he was dissociating from who he was. There was an alienation, another thing he couldn't describe to Deepanshu, and Harneet didn't get it either. He knew she would in the future, when she was here, and they could speak about their lives the way they did back in Jalandhar.

Thinking of her made him pull out his phone and scroll down to her name on WhatsApp. It was early evening in India, and she wouldn't respond because she would be home with her parents. He clicked on her profile picture and stared, the slim girl standing beside a tree, wearing some kind of uniform. She had told him it was taken on a school trip years ago. He felt an urge to caress her profile picture but didn't because he imagined everyone around him peeking. When he looked up, no one was staring. Pulling out his earphones, he switched to YouTube, selecting a playlist of religious songs made the week before he left Jalandhar.

Deepanshu still listened to the same brash pop, but Sukhpreet found it increasingly hard to summon enthusiasm for the music. The singers were engaged in an elaborate act of deception. He resented them and what they were doing, thinking of young men across the Punjab watching these gyrating figures on sports cars singing about how great it was in Canada.

Outside, the skies took on a brighter hue, the glare lighting up tiny homes that appeared on the horizon. Sukhpreet thought it strange how everyone who owned a home in this province of Ontario could be described as a millionaire. It reminded him of what one of his roommates in college had told him, about some village in Nabha or Bathinda, where every second farmer owned a Mercedes-Benz despite the villages having no proper roads. They had laughed at the time, but he thought, now, of how it must feel to homeowners here, cut off from the city in million-dollar homes. He wanted to sit down with them and ask what it meant to be rich in a rich country, and if it made them happy. He wanted to know if they felt an urge to leave their homes and travel, to uproot and transplant themselves the way he and people like him had.

He knew, by now, that these conversations would never happen. There were just three or four white professors in his college, and none spoke to the students unless they were compelled to. Their interactions were shallow and transactional, their presence paid for, and valued only for the validation they brought to that institution. Sukhpreet couldn't express this but had grown to recognize that he would always be looked at as an outsider. Increasingly, on trips to the city, he could sense an underlying hostility as well. 'They can hate us all they like, but we're not going anywhere,' Deepanshu had said, when he mentioned it one night. But why aren't we going, he wanted to ask, even though he knew the answer. He knew the hope that compelled him and everyone like him to stay—the hope of finding out what it meant to belong, the way they had once thought they could in the land that birthed them.

There was a devotional song playing, the third on his playlist. He hadn't been paying attention and felt guilty. These were songs his mother would sing when he was little, and he wished he could listen to them with her again. Suddenly, he grew upset at the impatience with which he had treated her. It was something his brother had done too, before he disappeared, and he saw what that must have done to this woman—this slow act of dismissal from the only people she loved.

The playlist was made to last the journey to and from Toronto, and reached the halfway mark as the train approached the city. He removed his earphones, and watched the compartment come slowly to life around him. The young men moved towards their bicycles and began checking their phones, and there was chatter about tips that suggested an easy familiarity. It reminded him of Deepanshu and the years he had spent doing the same thing, taking a train to the city before delivering food by bicycle for hours. He saw why his cousin had never told him the truth and was sad to realize it wouldn't have changed his decision. He would have come to Brampton anyway, armed with his confidence of being able to do better. Who was to say these men didn't have the same blind belief?

Stepping off at Bloor, he made his way towards the exit that would take him to Line 1, where another train would carry him five stops to Eglinton. The convenience store was less than a kilometre from the station, which he was thankful for, as he thought of commuting after September, when the temperature would drop. Fifteen minutes later, he stepped out at Eglinton and breathed in deeply. He thought of his journey, from a village where cows roamed muddy, unpaved streets, and where one in three homes had no running water. He imagined himself making his way confidently alongside a throng of people like him, from all corners of the globe, who had converged on this street in North America. For a moment, it felt as if he had done something right by leaving his home, his mother and country.

He walked slowly, trying not to reach the store before his shift began. The owner would insist on him beginning the minute he walked in, and it would be almost 2 p.m. before his half-hour lunchbreak in the back room. Deepanshu had promised to ask his supervisor about vacancies at the gas station where he worked; in the meantime, Sukhpreet kept applying to sundry jobs every night. The only options that presented themselves involved manual labour. He didn't know if the college would issue a diploma to someone who hadn't attended classes for a year, so the only way to stay on in Canada was to find employment that would allow him to apply for a Temporary Foreign Worker Program. It was how Deepanshu had stuck on before seeking a Permanent Residency. If Sukhpreet could do that, he would be able to travel home and meet his mother. They could then consider the possibility of her visiting him, which Deepanshu had yet to accomplish with his own parents.

As he approached the corner that would take him down a street to the store, he pictured a series of stepping stones, each marked with a target, stretching into the distance like a bridge across an ocean. At the far end, a horizon he couldn't determine, and a home in Canada, with a wife and children, his mother seated before a fireplace, looking out of a window at the snow coming down.

The owner of Gold Coin Convenience Store looked up as he pushed open the door, his presence announced by a bell. He nodded at him, then pointed to a stack of cardboard boxes placed haphazardly at the back in an aisle between candy and snacks. The store also functioned as a drop-off point for courier companies. Customers would come in, present proof of their identity, and collect what had been dropped off. Sukhpreet walked into the back room and put down his bag. It was 10.20 a.m. and he was early, but the owner wouldn't care, so he began sorting the packages and clearing the aisle. He made a mental note to walk more slowly the next morning.

As the day progressed, he moved mechanically from one task to the next. There were cartons to be opened and shelves to be filled, after which he would have to wipe down the insides of a large refrigerator. If the owner stepped away for lunch, he would step in behind the counter as a cashier, before going back to stacking products, helping customers find what they needed, and cleaning up spills or muddy footprints. The owner never spoke. He simply pointed at things and stared if he saw Sukhpreet idle. He had only spoken during his interview, and through the first couple of weeks whenever he needed something done. Sukhpreet knew he was a good employee because there had been no complaints but recognized the helplessness of his position. He needed the job, and the owner knew this too. He could withhold his pay or delay it, and nothing could be done.

It sometimes felt as if his brain shut down in those hours at the store, as if he transformed into a machine ticking off tasks mechanically, primed to repeat them day after day. To stop and think about it made him feel weak, so he refused, even on the ride back home when the only other people in the compartment were exhausted immigrants like him, or white Canadians on their way home from a party, or concert, or hockey game. He would watch them laugh, in their pretty dresses or team T-shirts, and wonder how they looked at him, or if they looked at all.

A little after 8 p.m., he retrieved his bag, before wishing the owner a good night. By his calculations, he had put in an extra hour, for which he wouldn't be paid. Deepanshu would laugh. It was still early in India, and he checked his phone for messages as he walked towards Eglinton. There was just one, from Harneet, informing him that her applications had been submitted. Her parents had insisted on her applying to two universities in the UK, along with two in Toronto. It must have been difficult for her to convince them, given that she had closer relatives in Birmingham than Canada, but maybe a college in Toronto would cost less. If she made it, perhaps he could speak to her parents a year from now.

There it was again, he thought, another stepping stone in the dark. A better job, more money, a larger room or separate condominium he could rent by himself, more savings to help his mother pay off her mortgage. It made him feel like a figure standing at the foot of a mountain, its summit obscured by clouds. Why couldn't he tell Harneet the truth about Canada, and what it meant to be a student? Why couldn't he save her from the worthlessness that would undoubtedly engulf her the way it had swallowed him? She would come expecting something and, if he really cared, he still had time to tell her the truth. He put away his phone without responding to her message. He would say nothing because it was selfishness that drove his deception. He needed her, and wanted to tell her that, and he believed, like his cousin did, that they could work together to create something bigger than themselves.

At Eglinton, he swiped his Presto card and walked down the stairs, waiting for a train going South. It would be past 10 p.m. before he got home, just as Deepanshu would be on his way out. Stepping into the half-empty train, he found a seat and leaned back. His feet ached, and he felt a keen longing for his mother. He remembered her rubbing his feet down with warm mustard oil when he was little, on days when his father would take both his sons to the fields and show them how to thresh wheat. They had no combine harvester, so everything was done manually. He looked at the compartment, trying to imagine how his father would have seen it, this life so alien from his own.

'Get the fuck off my seat,' said someone to the right, startling him. He turned in shock to see an older white man beside him. He wore a blue T-shirt spattered with stains and a Toronto Blue Jays cap, and held a can of something. Sukhpreet could smell alcohol and assumed he was homeless. There were a few other people in the compartment, but no one looked towards him. 'Get off my fucking seat, asshole,' the man said again, and Sukhpreet stood up hurriedly. He decided to step off at the next station even though Bloor was still two stops away. There was no one he could approach, and he moved towards the door, hoping the train would stop soon. 'Fucking Indians everywhere,' the man said loudly behind him. 'Go back to your fucking country.'

Sukhpreet didn't look back. He was embarrassed and wanted to run, but forced himself to stay calm. As the train stopped at Summerhill, he stepped off, hoping the man wouldn't follow. He kept walking until the train began to move. Then, breathing heavily, he turned and watched it gather speed and disappear into the subway tunnel. He knew there were drunks on the TTC. Deepanshu had warned him often, reminding him not to say a word to them, but this was the first time he had seen such naked hostility. He thought he would cry and blinked rapidly, waiting for the next train. The journey home passed without him noticing anything, and he walked into the condominium just as his cousin was leaving.

'Good news,' Deepanshu said, standing up as Sukhpreet entered their bedroom. 'What's wrong?' he asked, and Sukhpreet shook his head.

'Nothing, just a lot of work today. What's the good news?'

'No vacancy at the gas station, but there may be something better than your job at the store. My boss rents a place in Toronto and the building next to his is looking for an assistant to the superintendent. He says it was an urgent posting and thinks you may get it because he knows the manager. They were neighbours in Colombia.'

'How do I apply as an assistant superintendent without any experience?'

'They want someone with little experience because the pay is low, but it won't be minimum wage, and you get an employment letter. Apply tomorrow and just take it. That letter acts as proof of employment, so we can get our own place. Let's talk in the morning. I'm going to be late.'

Sukhpreet laughed.

'What's so funny?' Deepanshu asked.

'The job. They call them supers.'

'What?'

'Superintendents. They call them "super" in Canada. I know someone who will find that very funny.'

Rubbing his arm affectionately, Deepanshu walked out.

'Where is the job?' Sukhpreet asked.

'Not far from your store,' Deepanshu replied. '640 Rosebud Avenue. Check Google Maps. You'll get it because my boss says you will. I have a good feeling about this.'

He didn't wait for a reply and left. Sukhpreet sat on the bed and pulled out his phone. Clicking the maps icon, he typed in the address.

TORONTO

12 SEPTEMBER 2019

It was uncanny how Woody seemed to know when something wasn't right. Maynard had set an alarm for 5.30 a.m., which must have been enough of a sign that this was no ordinary day, but he had noticed it the night before too, when the dog had refused to leave his sight, following him around the condo. He bent down. 'It's okay, buddy, it's going to be okay.' Woody looked up, whining softly. After a while, Maynard lay back again and closed his eyes. He slept in fits and starts these days, falling asleep on some afternoons and waking up in the early evening, his mouth open. He had slipped into bed at 10 p.m. the night before but hadn't dozed off until 2 a.m. Yawning, he rubbed his eyes, wondering how bloodshot they were.

How would the day end? He had no idea if he would come back to Woody. He had considered taping a handwritten note to his computer with instructions on where the dog could go, but had abandoned the idea because he had no clue. Who would take Woody and where did they place dogs whose owners were unreachable? Sitting up again, he looked at his dog in silence.

It still felt unreal how they had arrived at this point. How had he allowed himself to be evicted? Diego had no choice but to let him go because of how obviously unfit he was for physical labour, but he couldn't help feeling as if the superintendent had relished giving him the news, knowing what it would mean.

It was still dark outside, but he didn't turn on the lamp. It had been three months since he had lost the job, and eleven weeks since the letter from Beltway Properties informing him that they had initiated eviction proceedings. There were people on Reddit urging him to file a lawsuit, and that he could hold out for a few more months, but even asking a lawyer for advice cost money. He had lost, and everyone knew it.

All he could do, now, was send a message. Diego was not an option. He was taller, more powerful and could hurt him. It had to be the younger man, that skinny immigrant who had taken his job. He had watched him from the window, pushing dustbins across the parking lot, picking up cartons of soda. Their paths had crossed a few times as he walked Woody downstairs, and he had never looked him in the face, making sure his cap was pulled down low.

It was hard to imagine someone so slight being able to do what he couldn't, but that was what they all did, the immigrants. They crept in, pushing themselves to the limit, until they had a foot in the door. It was only a matter of time before this young man settled in and took over. Diego was a fool to think his position was safe, and that the company wouldn't replace him with cheaper labour. The immigrant was probably paid by the hour, with no benefits, but he wouldn't complain. They all did it without a word, until the day they were allowed inside, and then something would flip. He could almost picture it, the brown kid in Diego's office, ignoring Maynard's presence a year from now, treating him the way Diego did. It was unforgivable, a country ready to cast him aside and watch him slip into homelessness because there were outsiders more worthy of a place at the table.

He stood up, the sudden movement making Woody sit up too. He was agitated and needed to calm down. The boy would be here in a few hours, and he needed the element of surprise. Without it, there was no telling how the attack would go. He could be hurt badly, and that would not do. It had to be swift, and efficient, and he had to be back before anyone spotted him. The stairways were empty on most mornings, with residents choosing the elevators, but there was no way of knowing. He breathed in deeply and counted to twenty. He had read somewhere about how this could slow down one's heart rate. He thought of Googling it, then changed his mind.

Walking into the living room, he checked the time. A little under four hours before the boy began mopping. He had tracked his schedule for two weeks, leaving the door open until he could hear him on the stairway with his bucket and mop. He wasn't always on time, but Maynard had a good idea of when the floors were to be swabbed. He wished he could take a nap, if only to feel a little less enervated. His body was leaden, as if he had eaten too much. Lack of sleep coupled with the stress of figuring out his next move. He hoped it would be several hours before they figured out who the attacker was.

Woody had followed him and was whining again. Maynard stepped into the kitchen. He filled the electric kettle before opening the dog food. There was half a bag left, which would be enough for a couple of days. Woody would be taken care of by whoever took charge of pets when their owners weren't available. He hoped it would be someone kind, and looked down, his eyes suddenly wet with tears. Turning on the stove, he placed two slices of bread on a pan and waited for it to heat up, while Woody ate his breakfast.

He hummed as the bread began to brown. It was a song he vaguely remembered his mother singing, although it could just as well be something played on the speakers at Canadian Tire. Woody continued to eat as Maynard picked up the bread and placed it on a plate, applying a generous scrape of butter across each slice. Pouring hot water from the kettle into a mug, he dropped in a tea bag and took the plate. Then, looking at the bread, he put it down and applied more butter. 'Why skimp, eh?' he said, loudly.

Woody had finished eating and followed him into the living room. Switching on the computer, Maynard ate as the monitor came to life. When he was done, he came back with tea, sipping it as he clicked on the Microsoft Word icon.

'*I AM NOT A WHITE SUPREMACIST*' it read in bold capitals at the top of the document he had created the night before. 'Good headline for the CBC and those lefties at the Star,' he said to himself, as he scrolled through what he had written.

> My name is Maynard Wilson. I am fifty-two years old, and I live in Toronto. I was born and raised in Orillia and moved to this city when I was twenty-five. I have lived at 640 Rosebud Avenue in unit 204 since 2012. I am writing this letter to inform you that no matter what the press and fake newspapers and fake

news say about me none of it is true. I want to tell you why I did it so you do not judge me based on what the so-called journalists will print when I have been silenced.

We have all been silenced. Canadians like me whose parents and grandparents built this great country. We have been silenced and continue to be silenced but I have had enough. I will not be told to shut up and I will not disappear. By the time you read this I may be in jail. I will not run and I have no idea if they will allow me to make a statement.

I decided to harm that man to make a point to the prime minister and the rest of those thugs sitting in Ottawa. My point is simple: *Enough is enough*.

You cannot just bring in more and more immigrants without fixing the problems of Canadians first. I may be homeless in a month. How? How come an honest Canadian born and raised in this country can find no employment and no means of earning enough to pay rent and buy food for a dog? I have no wife or family, and I cannot take care of myself. How are other Canadians going to find a home or buy groceries, and how are they going to survive if you keep bringing in more people without checking to see if we are okay first?

There are no jobs and no homes, and not enough doctors. Grocery bills rise every month. Do you know how much a loaf of bread costs these days? $4. My father used to buy enough to feed us for a month on less than $50. What are Canadians supposed to eat?

I don't want to kill that man. I am saying this because I want you to believe it. I want to hurt him, but I make no promises. If he dies, his blood is on your hands not mine. It is on the ministers who allowed him to come here. It is on the media that will only listen if some immigrant gets hurt. You didn't give me a choice.

If the media says I was a hateful person who was driven by helplessness or anger that is not true. I am struggling with financial problems, this is not about that. This is about taking control of my life and hoping it inspires other Canadians to do the same. I am just a guy who loves his country.

I have to also say that I do not know this man I will be accused of harming. He may be a decent guy but all I see is someone who shouldn't be here taking our jobs. My EI doesn't cover rent because of people like this guy who come here on visas that shouldn't allow them to work. This guy will bring his parents here and they will get free healthcare and there will just be more and more people.

It has to stop. I am using him as my messenger. Maybe that is the only way. I have nothing more to say. Please print my statement in full without removing anything and without changing anything to suit your lefty biases and your commie bullshit.

One last thing is about my dog Woody who is sweet and kind and gentle. I hope he finds a good home with someone who will take care of him. On this computer is a document with information about his veterinarian and the medication he needs as he recovers from surgery.

Canada First.

Maynard Wilson
12 September 2019

He read it again, his lips moving as the tea grew cold on the table. Woody barked, then lay down. Maynard stretched out his arms, then folded them and looked around the room. 'No more questions for today, please speak to my attorney,' he said.

Checking the bottom right of the screen, he saw that an hour had passed since he had woken up. He yawned, then walked to the bedroom. Woody followed and sat beside the bed, as Maynard climbed in and lay down. He set an alarm again, for two hours later, and fell asleep. Outside, the sky began to turn, light leaching softly upwards from the horizon. There was no sound of birds, with most of the robins gone. Maynard snored softly with his back turned away from the window.

At 8.30, the alarm went off and he sat up in panic. Checking his watch, his shoulders slumped. 'Almost time, buddy,' he said in a low voice, stepping off the bed as Woody walked out before him and waited by the door. Going to the kitchen for a second cup of tea, Maynard carried it to the window and stared out at the empty parking lot. His building faced a row of townhouses. He sipped, staying at the window until he was finished. When he was done, he rinsed the mug and placed it on a plastic mat to dry.

'Time to get dressed,' he said to Woody and walked to the small bedroom closet. Pushing aside a row of checked shirts, he reached out to the back and pulled out a red hoodie. Sniffing it, he coughed, dusting it lightly with his other arm. He pulled it on and smoothed down the front, his palms on a maple leaf embossed in white. 'I look like a bloody tourist,' he said, softly. 'Maybe they'll think it was one.' He picked up a faded blue cap, embellished with a logo that was no longer decipherable, and pulled it down low before walking out to the living room.

Logging into Reddit, he looked for the official community for r/Canada. 'Today is the day' he typed. 'Patriots, we are ready to take over. Watch the news coming out from Toronto. Warning: Liberals are not gonna like what they see.' Clicking the 'post' button, he leaned back, wondering what responses would come in. He half expected the moderators to remove his message immediately, but nothing happened.

At 9.30 a.m., he switched off the computer. 'Stay here,' he said to Woody, walking to the door and staring out the peephole. There was no sound. Diego's assistant must have entered the building by now and was probably on his way up the stairs.

'This is it, buddy,' he said to Woody. 'Wish me luck.' Opening the door, he slipped out.

CODA

He was cold, colder than he had ever been. The air was still, like the ponds of Chukhiara in winter, when the water would turn dark and sluggish.

Sukhpreet sensed nothing but a chill that lay at the centre of his being, expanding slowly outward. Fleeting images came to him, in black and white, and in colour, of places and people he knew but could no longer recognize. He watched them appear as if on a big screen playing to an empty theatre. Slow down, he wanted to say, but his lips did not move.

Then it was dark, and the minutes passed, or hours.

There were pictures again, of a woman he had always known, only now she seemed younger. He saw a man who looked just like him, and two little boys, and fields that shimmered the way sunlight would dance on the surface of pools. There was a girl in pigtails climbing into a bus, and lithe men in turbans riding bicycles, and now they were dancing on a street that stretched into the distance, with buildings on both sides that rose and vanished into an unbearably blue sky.

He wanted to reach out and touch them all. There was so much to say.

And then it was cold again, and black, and silence fell upon the world like a shroud.

ACKNOWLEDGEMENTS

Many thanks to Dharini Bhaskar and her colleagues at HarperCollins India: Bonita Vaz-Shimray for the beautiful cover, Naiyya Singh for help with marketing, and Wesley D'Souza for the careful edits. Thanks also to my agent, Kanishka Gupta.

I am also indebted to Jerry Pinto, Santanu Bhattacharya, and Sonia Faleiro, who gave me their time, and whose words of encouragement have meant a lot to me.

ABOUT THE AUTHOR

Lindsay Pereira was born and raised in Bombay. He studied at St. Xavier's College and the University of Mumbai and holds a PhD in literature for his work on gender attitudes implicit in nineteenth-century Indian fiction.

He was co-editor with the late Eunice de Souza of *Women's Voices: Selections from Nineteenth and Early Twentieth Century Indian Writing in English*. His first novel, *Gods and Ends*, was shortlisted for the 2021 JCB Prize for Literature and Tata Literature Live! First Book Award for fiction. His second novel, *The Memoirs of Valmiki Rao*, was longlisted for the 2024 Crossword Book Award for fiction, and won the Mumbai Literature Live! Literary Award for fiction book of the year. A collection of his short stories, *Songs Our Bodies Sing*, was published in 2025.